15.8.20

If you find it
please take
it, and t
you've fin[ished]... [le]ave
it for someone else
to enjoy.

Please post a photo
Always
on social media (if you
have it), when you've
found me, and use
the following hashtags:

LUCY ONIONS'

#ibelieveinbookfairies
#lucyonionsauthor
#blackdreampublishing
Can you also tag the
place you've found me?

ISBN: 978-1-9163441-2-9

DEDICATION

To Simon and Molly, Mom and Dad, Ella, Paul, Max and Harry. I love you, always.

You don't know me, but I know you. Very well. I know your favourite film is The Crow, your favourite band, Pearl Jam. You were devastated when David Bowie died.

You feed Norm at seven am, before you leave for work. I know he won't go out if it's raining or even a little bit windy. He's not the best guard-dog, but then you didn't rescue him for that reason.

How do I know all this? I just do. I make it my business to, to know all there is to know, about you, about your life. I love you, Iris. I'll love you always.

1

1

I stare at the note in my hand in shock. It's weird. I don't feel scared, I just, I don't know.

Norm's whimpering, looking up at me with those big bloody eyes. He wants to go for his walk. He's frustrated, and I can't say I blame him. I'm stood here, in front of him, his collar and lead dangling from the crook of my elbow.

"Sorry, mate," I tell him, and he cocks his head to one side, signaling his understanding, and disappointment.

Maybe the walk would do me good, give me a chance to think. All I have to do is move, just put one foot in front of the other. Walk. My mind does not want to play ball, though. It's not letting me move.

Norm barks.

"Stop it, Norm!"

He knows exactly what I'm saying, and he ambles away from me, huffing and puffing in the way only disappointed dogs know how.

I swallow the last gulp of red wine, finishing the bottle. I could open another one, but I know I won't just stop at one extra glass. It's a waste, isn't it? Might as well drink the whole bloody thing. It's Saturday night. There's no work tomorrow. Sod it!

I turn the note over and over in my hands. Maybe if I do it enough, the sender's name will magically appear. No. No magic tonight.

I pick up my phone and look at the time. I'm wearing my watch, but for some stupid reason, I think it's easier to press a button than to turn my left wrist around. Ten thirty. God, it feels later than that.

I head to the kitchen and grab a bottle of Cabernet Sauvignon. I fill my glass almost to the top, which leaves just over half of the dark, claret liquid left in the green-tinted bottle. I've got the munchies, and the only thing that's going to satisfy my alcohol-induced hunger, is the posh bag of salt-and-vinegar crisps that I bought on my way back from work yesterday. I pour the entire contents into a large bowl. Greedy? Hell yes. Do I give a shit? No.

There's nothing on the tv, well, nothing worth watching anyway. I mean, what's that all about? It's the weekend, for heaven's sake. But then, I suppose it's because the big bosses of all these bloody channels assume that everyone has a social life. And I say to that, No, you are wrong! Social life? What's that?

Occasionally, it does bother me that I don't get asked to go out every weekend. But, for the most part, I'm happy to veg out in front of the television, or in tonight's case, with a book in hand. I don't need to go out and get trashed and feel like shit the next day. Some might think it sad. If it is, I don't want to be happy. Staying-in is the new going-out, anyway. Apparently. I do make an exception for gigs though, so I suppose I'm not a total hermit.

I'm trying to settle. I need to so that I can enjoy my book. But it's no use. I won't rest until I find out who sent this note.

2

I wonder what she's thinking, right now. She's home. I know that much. If only I could be a fly on the wall. If only I could see her face.

This is just the start. The toe in the water. I have so many plans. This is going to be fun.

3

I love Sundays. Not that I need an excuse to sit in my pajamas all day, but Sunday is the one day it just feels right. I've no plans, other than to read, listen to my records, cook a small, roast dinner (for two. Norm loves his dinners), and drink wine. Again.

It's seven pm, and time to indulge in another Sunday ritual.

The sound of water gushing from the taps is making me tired. I'm staring at the flow of it, and it's mesmerising. My eyes start to sting, so I blink, snap myself out of my reverie. I pour bath milk into the cascading water, and watch bubbles develop where it hits.

My glass of wine sits next to my current read, on the wooden bath caddy I treated myself to last Christmas. Best thing I've ever bought, apart from Norm, that is. It comes a pretty close second.

I disrobe, hang my dressing gown on the hook on the back of the bathroom door. The temperature of the water takes my breath away, makes my toe, then foot, recoil. Only momentarily, mind you. My breath catches a few more times, until I settle down, fully submerging myself, in the gorgeous smelling, steaming liquid.

4

I love Sundays.

Her bathroom window is steamed up. It always is around this time, on this day.

Imagination is a powerful thing, and I'm imagining exactly what I could do to her, right now.

ALWAYS

5

I t is so, so cold. The air around me feels thick, and wet. I can feel it seeping into me. That's what I get for coming out in just my coat. What was I thinking? I really should have put my beanie on, and my gloves. But no, any ideas of practicality must have been left on my pillow in the struggle to leave my bed. Just around the corner now though. Not long to go.

I pull the swivel chair out from my desk and sigh. Christ, I hate Mondays. I hate them as much as I adore Sundays. What happens over the weekend that warrants all this paperwork? It's ridiculous.

I hang my denim jacket up on my coat hook and take my headphones off. I switch on my computer and ponder what I'm going to do for lunch. How can I be hungry already?

There's already a queue forming in the kitchen, my co-workers lining up before me. There's only one thing on all of our minds. Coffee. I could go back to my desk and wait until it's died down, but it never does. These people I work with, they truly are addicted to it.

As always, I'm at the back of the line. I should have just

11

kept my headphones on. Anything's better than staring at the backs of the people I work with.

We're an antisocial bunch. We'd all be stuffed on one of those team-building days. To be fair, I'm happy just to do my work and go home. There are a few people, of the twenty on this floor, that I'd like to get to know a bit better. A few that interest me. A few who seem like they're cut from the same cloth as me. One day, I'm sure I'll pluck up the courage to speak to George, Lucas and Adam. Yes, all men. I can't help it if I get on with the opposite sex more than my own. Someday, I will speak to them, but for now, I'll just admire them from afar.

I'm up next for a caffeine kick. I stare blankly at the brown, steaming liquid that fills my cup. I zone out at work far more than I should. It doesn't take a lot. My head is a far more exciting place to inhabit.

I amble back to my desk, sit down and take a deep breath, preparing to tackle this paper mountain in front of me. I pick up the first file, yet another book submission that screams all style yet no substance. Occasionally, you'll get a manuscript that blows you away, that leaves you speechless. You have to plough through a lot of shit to find a diamond.

I open the file and start taking down the particulars. Name, age, bio. I've read the same dross over, and over. Can they not come up with something more original?

I flick to the next page, and my eye catches something drop from the file, onto my lap.

It's another note.

6

I know she's got it. The look on her face is enough to tell me that.

She's reading it. Well, I say reading. Her eyes flit and flicker over it, and she folds it up quickly. Now she knows that the person sending her these notes works here, in this office.

I'm not doing this to scare her. I've loved her since the moment I saw her walk through those doors, on her first day. I've never fallen for anyone so quickly, and so hard. I don't know whether I particularly like the feeling, but then again, maybe I do. Why would I be doing this if I didn't?

I'm not the most confident person. In fact, I shy away from anything that draws attention to me. This is the only way I can do this, the only way I can connect with her. Eventually, she will know who I am. It's going to take some time, but she will.

Good things come to those who wait.

7

Iris,

Now you know how I know you. I walk past you every day at work. And I know what you're thinking. You're thinking that your secret admirer (because, honestly, that is what I am) obviously does more than walk past you. I'm not going to lie because I would never do that to you, you deserve to know the truth.

I respect you too much to not be honest with you. I follow you, everywhere. I don't do it because I want to frighten you. I do it because I care. I want to make sure you get home, safely. Once you're through that door, I go my own way. Well, most of the time. Some of the time.

I have to be honest though, Iris, I would do anything to cross the threshold because I've actually been invited to.

Oops, too much information.

xxx

8

No. No way. So, did this *stalker* just slip the last note through my letterbox? Or has he, or she, been in my house? Put the letter there to look as though it had been delivered?

I keep reading, and rereading. I should be freaking out, shouldn't I? I should be frightened, scared. And I suppose I am, a little. What I am is angry! Angry and somewhat intrigued.

I stand up, allow my eyes to traverse the room, skimming the tops of workstations. I don't know what I hope to find. It's not like the phantom-note-writer is going to wave at me, is it? *Oh hi, Iris. The note? Yes, all my handiwork!* It's not like I'm a bloody body-language expert either. Everyone looks busy. Everyone is working. I am not, and if I don't knuckle down and get sorted soon, I'll have the boss on my back.

I sit back down and pick the manuscript back up, turn the page and feel my eyes glaze over as soon as I read the first sentence of the synopsis. I swear to God, if I read another one of these generic, vampire-romance novels, I'm going to jack. Don't get me wrong, they sell, and they sell well, but where's the originality these days? Why can't these new authors just think before they send this stuff in? Because they know. They know there's a market for it. The day I get a manuscript of this genre though, that's as fresh as it is dark, and unique, I'll throw a bloody party. Admittedly, I'll probably be the only one there to celebrate.

What a surprise. Once again, I'm eating lunch in the darkest, quietest corner of the staff room. My lunchbox is about as exciting as a coffin. If I had my head screwed on, I'd be organised, plan and prepare my meals in advance. I'd take my time to make them appealing. But I don't. I'm pretty lazy like that.

I can't wait to tuck into my soft-cheese covered rice-cakes, stick of celery and pack of raisins. That's a lie. I have a feeling it's not going to be a taste explosion.

You'd think, what with reading all day (I'm still amazed that I get paid to do it), that I'd not want to read for myself, for pleasure. But reading is my life, it really is. I don't go anywhere without a book, and I never leave the house without at least a couple of pens and a notebook (I have many. I'm slightly obsessed with them). I know I have a story in me, somewhere. Without sounding too big-headed, but if some of the shit I'm reading at work, on almost a daily basis, is anything to go by, my book (whenever I get around to finishing it) will be nothing short of wonderful. Nothing wrong with being modest.

I put my headphones on, close my eyes and circle my thumb on the clicking wheel of my mp3 player. I open them to see I've landed on The Used. I set all tracks to shuffle, let my book drop open on my lap, and for a whole hour, I can disappear.

9

She does the same thing, day in, day out. Sits in that corner, clearly in her own little world. I wonder what music is filling her head. This is where I need to step up my game. I need to find out what stuff she's into.

She must read at a frantic pace because she's got a new one on the go pretty much every other day.

It's the easiest, and best, time to watch her. She never looks up from whatever book she's devouring along with her lunch. I don't have to worry about being caught out.

She looks so beautiful, and I know it's not the nicest habit, but the way she chews her nails when she gets to a particularly gripping part of her book, it's just so cute.

I smile as she darts up from the well-worn, leather armchair, cursing under her breath as she rushes past me, realising it's time to get back to reality.

LUCY ONIONS

10

Only an hour to go now. An hour until I am out of this place. I know that must sound like I hate my job, but I don't. Really, I don't. I love it. I just can't seem to gel with anyone here. I've tried, I really have. The girls have absolutely no time for me. I kind of get that. I'm not like them, not at all. I know you shouldn't judge a book by its cover (Ha! See what I did there?), but I have absolutely nothing in common with them.

George, Adam and Lucas. They're a whole other story (I'm doing it again). They look exactly like the kind of people I could get on with. It helps that they're a little easy on the eyes too.

Their workstations mirror mine. They've made them their own, like I've done with mine. Posters of bands and stickers adorn the partition walls. Screensavers of their favourite music artists. Assorted miniature toys. You can really tell a lot about someone based on what their work space looks like.

I will approach them, in one way or another. One day. I just need to grow a pair. It's just talking. What is there to be scared of?

The Dirty Duck is heaving as I walk past it. I glance quickly through the steamed-up windows. There's a band on, or at least it sounds like there's going to be. I can tell a soundcheck a mile off – I've been involved in more than I can count, with all the bands I've been in over the years.

I shouldn't go in. I should go straight home. And anyway, I'm not prepared. I'm not ready. It's a Monday night and I would be breaking one of my cardinal rules – no merriment on a school night. I never go out when I know I've got work the next day. Hell, I never go out. Some invisible force seems to be pulling me towards the door though. I should fight it…

I'm going in. It's about time I started to branch out. I haven't got to go mad. If I stick to beer rather than wine, I'll be fine.

The smell of body odour, hops, and malt hits me as I open the door. Heat rushes at me, envelops me. I realise I may be the smallest person in here as I squeeze past bodies of all shapes and sizes. I'm barely reaching the shoulders of the men around me. The floor is tacky with years upon years of spilled beer and God knows what else.

I wedge myself in between a couple of guys at the bar. They're oblivious to my presence, talking loudly, well, practically shouting, at each other. I'm losing patience quickly. I mean, come on, surely they can feel there's a whole other person sardined between them.

They look down as I give them a gentle nudge and make room for me. No quibble, no snide remarks. The guy to my right is being served, and when the barmaid gives him his drinks, he gestures to me, tells her I'm next. This isn't so bad after all.

I order a pint of beer and wind myself through the throng of Monday night revelers. I'm surprised that so many people are out, but then, this is all very foreign to me. Maybe tonight is the night to change that. Maybe tonight is the night I'll actually make a friend. Baby steps.

There's a small cloakroom to my left. I'll put my stuff in there. Get rid of my baggage for an hour or so.

I see movement behind a heavy, black curtain, hanging at the back of a full, drum-kit, and then Adam, George and Lucas walk on to stage. I feel my cheeks flush a little. This is quite unexpected. George looks straight at me, gently waves his hand and smiles.

LUCY ONIONS

11

S hit. She's here. Smiling at me. She looks uncomfortable, but then I suppose I would be too if the shoe was on the other foot. Iris never goes out. Ever. I've followed her enough to be certain of that.

I can't lie, I'm nervous now. I'm always a little anxious before a gig, but the feeling passes as soon as we hit the stage. This has thrown a spanner in the works though, Iris being here. Her eyes will be on us, on me. I can't fuck up, not tonight. Maybe if I impress her enough, we'll finally get the chance to talk. Do I want that? Do I want to talk to her? I'm enjoying this game. I'm loving worshipping her from afar. The mystery of it all. The intrigue. The suspense. I like the idea that I'm ruffling her feathers, and I know it's a little sadistic, but there's something almost endearing about her when she seems frightened.

Adam's doing a quick line-check on the drums, Lucas checking his tuning. I pick up my bass and sling the strap around my neck. I nod at the guys, take a deep breath.

"One, two, three, four."

LUCY ONIONS

12

Of the three, I've always felt more drawn towards George. I know I've never spoken to him, and apart from glancing over at his workstation, I know nothing about him. Maybe that's the attraction. I can't lie, I do fantasise about him. More often that I should admit.

He's a beautiful man. So beautiful. And then there's his voice. I would never have imagined such a gruff, manly tone from him. It doesn't sit right with his looks, but then again, it's really endearing.

It's not just his speaking voice that's surprising. His vocals are blowing me away. Man, he can sing.

I'm starting to relax, and I'm warming to all of this. For three guys, they have an immense sound, and I am utterly transfixed as George looks at me again. I feel my cheeks blush.

13

She has not taken her eyes off me. I can see her from the corner of my eye. She's not even taken a single sip from her drink. Is she breathing?

It's the last song of the set, and I know I need to acknowledge her. We hit the last chord and I look straight at her, fuzzy feedback ringing in my ears. Wait, is she blushing? She is.

I thank the crowd, wish them goodnight. She scarpers, straight to the bar. I have to see what she orders. I'm going to buy her a drink.

With only three of us in the band, packing down is easy. The bar has its own PA – monitors, speakers – the whole shebang. It's literally a case of unplugging. That's why we love playing here. We play, and then we drink.

I can't. I can't approach her. I haven't got it in me.

LUCY ONIONS

14

I've got to do something. Got to make a move. I'm here now, we've seen each other. It's going to feel awkward if I don't say hello.

I'm not good at necking beer, but I do, and call in another. I'm watching the barmaid pull mine, and as I stare at the golden, amber liquid, filling the pint glass, I ask her to make it two. I haven't a clue what he drinks, but it's the thought, right?

He's chatting to Adam and Lucas, his back to me. It's going to look really bloody desperate if I walk straight up to them whilst they're talking. I'll just go and sit at the table at the front and wait for my moment. Can I do this? Have I got the balls? My hands are getting clammy with nerves, so I take a gulp of my beer to try and calm down.

I look up to see Adam and Lucas walking towards me. I am dumbstruck, and I hope it doesn't show. They say hello, you know, like normal people do, and I say hello back. Well, I say something that sounds like *hello* anyway. They tell me it's really good to see me, that it's nice to see me outside of work, and I feel like a weight has been lifted. They ask if I'm staying a while longer, and as much as my head is yelling *no*, my heart jumps in and tells me it's okay. I tell them I am, and they ask if

I want a drink. This is going far easier than I expected, and I could think of nothing better right now.

They tell me they'll be right back, that George is busy loading the gear into their van, and that he'll be with us shortly. I try my best at nonchalant, but I don't think it works, and as Adam and Lucas wander off towards the bar, I feel like a teenager all over again.

15

No choice now, the lads have spoken to her. It's going to look pretty weird if I don't join them for a drink. I can't crawl out of this one.

I lock the van and decide to leave it in the car park tonight. I'll leave the keys here, behind the bar (my Uncle owns this place, and this is just one of the many perks I enjoy). I'm going to want to sink a few tonight to help get me through this, and I have never, ever driven whilst under the influence. I'll just pick it up after work tomorrow. After I've followed Iris home. It won't take long.

She's sitting on her own, and although she doesn't look as uncomfortable as she did earlier, she's certainly not relaxed.

She's stunning. Pure. Her personality is as beautiful as she looks.

It's now or never. I breathe deeply and set a course to the table. She looks up at me, smiling widely. There's that blush again. I ask her if I can sit. She happily, quietly allows me to. I pull a chair out across from her, and I stare. I know I'm staring. I can't stop. She stares back. We don't speak. I could stare at her always, and never get tired of the view.

LUCY ONIONS

16

I can't take my eyes off him. His deep, brown eyes alternate between looking into mine, and then down at his hands.

I wonder if he can sense how stupidly nervous I am?

I'm thinking how good it must feel to kiss him. Would it be good? Would it be as perfect as it is in my head?

His dark brown, thick, slightly waved hair settles on broad, toned shoulders. The neck of his grey t-shirt just shows the top of his right collarbone, and I'm starting to feel a little hot under the collar myself. Anyone would think he'd just stripped off in front of me.

He's nervous too. I can tell.

Considering he's not long been off stage, he smells good. Really good. A damn sight better than half of the punters in here.

He brings his hands up from his lap and puts them, crossed, on the table. If the sight of his shoulders didn't scream that he's fit, that he clearly works out, looks after himself, his arms certainly give the game away. They're just the right kind of muscly, not too much, not too little.

I drag my eyes away from his arms and look back at his face. We're not speaking but this is the most we've ever communicated. It's sad, I suppose. We've worked in the same office for the last two years.

I want him to say something, anything. I want to hear that deep, velvety sound that sends a shiver through me every time he speaks. Jesus, listen to me! If I was reading this shit in a book, I'd be cringing by now.

Adam and Lucas are still nowhere near to ordering drinks. The crowd at the bar is at least four deep. I swallow the last of my beer and just when I seriously do not need to feel any more nervous, I burp. I can't help it. I cover my mouth just in time to stop me from feeling too mortified. I open my mouth to apologise and realise George is smiling at me.

17

She is so cute. Her face when she burped? Brilliant.

Adam comes up behind me, puts his arms around my shoulders. I can feel his chin resting on the top of my head. We've been the best of friends for eighteen years. First met in primary school. I'm pretty sure we were six. Five or six. Something like that. Lucas is a good friend too, really great guy, but me and Adam have got history.

By twenty-two, we'd pooled our resources and put a deposit down on our studio flat. It's out of town, so a bit easier on the bank account, and if we had got somewhere slap bang in the town centre, there'd be way too much temptation to piss our wages up the wall. It's nice to be far enough away to be out of it, but not so far that we can't come and do our gigs and party a little.

My best friend sits beside me, and not long after, Lucas shows up, balancing four pints on a tray

We each pick up our drinks in perfect unison.

Someone's going to have to break this ice.

LUCY ONIONS

18

I down half of my pint in a few mouthfuls. Dutch courage and all that.

"That was a great set," I say quietly.

George smiles and says thank you, says he's really glad I enjoyed it.

"I had no idea you three were in a band," I say, surprising myself with this new-found nerve, "how long have you been together?"

This is better. You're getting there now, kid. This is what's called conversation.

Adam explains that they don't tend to advertise it at work because they want to keep these two lives separate. That, and they're not all that keen on seeing certain people from work at their gigs. They've been playing together for six years.

George is staring again, his eyes silently boring into mine. I'm getting the feeling he's one of those kinds of people that could get himself into trouble as a result of over-staring. He doesn't do it on purpose, no, or I don't imagine he does. He's an observer, a people watcher. I'd love to know what he's thinking.

"Do you play here often?" I say, and immediately cringe at the cliché.

George's face cracks into a grin.

"You do realise that sounds like you're trying to chat us up?" he laughs. It's higher-pitched than his talking voice, sing-song like.

He's right. That's exactly what it sounds like. My cheeks are burning and the thought of making a quick exit is very appealing.

"Staying for another one, Iris?" he says, and just the sound of my name leaving his mouth stops me in my tracks. I want to stay, I actually, really want to, but…

"Um, no, I'm sorry. I need to get home and let my dog out. I usually take him for a walk after work, but I got a bit waylaid. Thanks for the offer though."

Did his face drop, just a little, ever so slightly? I take a deep breath, unsure if what I'm about to say is a good, or bad, thing.

"Maybe we could do this again another time. Weekends are best for me."

George's grin grows even wider.

"Sounds good to me."

19

I don't know why I was so bloody nervous. She's so cool. I think we both let our nerves get the better of us at first, but it's amazing how a bit of alcohol can loosen you up.

I just hope she means it, us meeting up again. She might have just said it to be polite, but I've wanted this for so long – to get to know Iris, properly.

I know I should stop following her, stop leaving the notes. But I love the thrill of it though, and I've got so used to, for want of a better word, stalking her, that losing that, letting it go, would mean losing a big part of my life. I know that sounds incredibly pathetic, but I can't help it.

I am obsessed.

Totally.

Utterly.

LUCY ONIONS

20

I am so, so glad I stopped drinking when I did last night. I'm feeling a bit cotton-headed as it is, and that's only after a few drinks. Any more, and I wouldn't have even stepped foot out of the house, let alone come in to work.

Work. I'm kind of dreading it. I know it's silly to feel that way. I know I don't need to. The ice has been broken now, at last. It should be a breeze to just waltz in and get on with my day, but if anything, I feel even more nervous than ever.

What I need to do is just go straight over to him. Strike while the iron is hot. Go and say hello to him before I even get chance to sit at my desk. If I don't do this, I won't speak to him at all.

LUCY ONIONS

21

"Morning, George," she says as she hangs up her jacket, "how are you feeling this morning?"

I've felt better. My head is pounding. I know I should have stopped drinking when Iris left, but I'm always buzzing after a gig and it takes ages for me to settle down. It'll teach me to try and keep gig bookings to weekends only. I can't handle hangovers. Not like I used to. Not anymore.

I tell her that I'm feeling a bit delicate and ask how she's feeling. She says she's glad she stopped when she did. I nod and tell her I should have done the same.

She laughs, tells me that she had a great night, that she really enjoyed it. She tells me that she's not being polite about it, and that she meant it when she suggested we go out again.

I'm so glad she's made the move. I mean, I would have spoken to her today, at some point, but it's really nice that she approached me first.

"Speak to you later then?" she says.

I watch her, the way her hips swish slightly as she walks away brings a smile to my dry mouth.

22

That wasn't so hard. Not hard at all. If anything, I enjoyed it. It's going to be so much easier now.

I pull my chair out from my desk, and, shock, horror, there are only three more manuscripts added to the one I left yesterday. That's what happens here. There's always an influx over the weekend, when the general public finally, after a long, busy week at work, get chance to do that last edit, and maybe one more, then attach their file to an email, and hit send.

I know how that feels, the elation, nerves, and relief, as you send your covering letter, synopsis and three-chapter sample for someone to pour over, and ultimately decide your fate. It's one of the reasons I love this job, most of the time. I've been there. Got the t-shirt.

Thanks to the staff who are happy to work the days that no one else wants to, everything gets sorted into genres, and then distributed to the relevant person. I'm Young Adult and Young Adult Fantasy although given the choice, I'd be working on Crime and Thriller.

The deluge of work becomes less, and less, as the week goes on, and then the cycle starts all over again on Monday. I mustn't grumble. I could think of far worse ways to make my money.

My stomach is rumbling, which is good timing as I'm about to go on my lunch break. I realise that in the rush to get out of the house this morning, I've forgotten the chicken salad that I'd got up half an hour earlier, just to prepare. Did I even take it out of the fridge? I hope not. Nothing worse than warm salad.

I grab my bag from under the desk and check that I have at least remembered my wallet. I have. Result.

I pull my coat off the hook it's been hanging on since I got here.

"You off out?" George asks, looking up at me.

"Forgot my lunch. Do you want anything while I'm out?"

What I should have said is, *do you fancy joining me?* But, alas, flirting isn't my forte.

"I'm okay, thanks for the offer though," he says.

I nod and open the door.

23

I should have just asked if I could join her. We could have had our lunch out. Together. I didn't leave her anything yesterday though, and I really fancy doing it today. Silver linings, I suppose.

I write the note quickly, but precisely, fold it into four, and get up from my chair. I walk the length of the room until I get to her workstation. Luckily, the small few who haven't scarpered to the staff room are fixated on their phone screens, whilst trying to eat their lunches.

That's one thing I love about Iris. She's not a slave to her phone. She's got a decent one, all singing and dancing, and I do see her on it from time to time, but at lunch time, she's always on her own, getting lost in whatever book she has in her hands.

I take one last, quick glance around to make sure no one is watching, and I sit. I'm pleasantly surprised by her choice of reading material. American Psycho is one of my all time favourites. I can't see a bookmark. Maybe she hasn't even started it yet. I open the book and leave the note between the copyright, and dedication pages. I want her to see it today. She has to. I've got to say, it's the best one yet.

LUCY ONIONS

24

You're going to tell him about us aren't you, Iris? You're going to tell him about the letters. You've got to. He deserves to know about your secret admirer.

Why don't you ever write back? Oh, you can't can you? Silly me. Kind of defeats the object of me being your secret admirer, doesn't it?

Just be straight with him. I'm sure he'd want you to. I've seen how cute you are together, all coy, and nervous.

Do you read these letters? I mean, really read them. Do you like getting them? I'd like to think you're keeping them somewhere safe.

I've studied you for so long now, and I've fallen for you. I'm sorry if this scares you. Then again, I'm not sorry.

I would love nothing more than to be with you, in every sense. I've thought about it, dreamt about it, more than you'll ever know. I could tell you, if you want. Tell you what I do to you in my dreams and fantasies. Maybe I could include all the details in my next letter? Maybe that would pique your interest a little more. Because I know you're already interested. I know you want to know who is sending these letters.

It could be anyone in this office. You have a lot of people to choose from. Men and women.

Hope you enjoyed your lunch.

25

I should report this. This is one sick, twisted joke, and I'm not finding it at all funny. To think that it's someone in this office who has been sending me these notes is making my stomach churn. It's pointless asking people because who the hell would own up to it? Would I admit to it if it was me sending out letters to one, or more, of my colleagues?

I can't even decipher the handwriting, something which I pride myself on. I know everyone's handwriting in this office. I've seen all the little margin notes, scribbles and sign-offs.

Should I mention all this to George? Should I show him the letters?

I fold the note up and put it with the other two, inside my notebook.

LUCY ONIONS

26

It's five pm and I still haven't got through these new, sci-fi manuscripts. Apart from putting all my effort into the note, I've dragged my backside all day, something that hasn't gone unnoticed by the boss. And now I've been *"asked"* to stay on until they're all processed. It's my own fault.

I watch everyone file out. Everyone except Iris. The two of us. All alone. Together.

Despite the size of the room, I feel oddly claustrophobic. I look at my computer monitor, pretend I'm hard at work.

"Haven't you got a home to go to?" she asks, walking towards me.

"Haven't you?"

I realise that that sounded harsh, and so I apologise for my abruptness.

"Don't worry. No offence taken," she says, and then looks at the pile on my desk, "ah, so that's why you're still here."

"In one."

"Do you need a hand? It would be nice to read through something different, Mr. Sci-Fi."

There's the flirting again. She's good at this.

"I thought you only did vampires and werewolves," I say,

hoping she realises I'm flirting back.

"They're okay, but I *do* so much more, you know?"

I feel my face redden, and I look down at my table. Anything to keep me from looking at her. Anything to stop her seeing what she's doing to me.

I hand her a manuscript. Our fingers brush on contact.

We read in silence, both of us scribbling notes as we go along.

"Wow. This is good," she says as she flips the last page.

"Yeah?"

"Yeah. Here, just take a look at this first paragraph," she offers, sidling right up next to me.

An awkward silence fills the air between us, and I feel my eyes widen instinctively.

I carry on reading. At least I try to. She's right, it's a great opener. Excellent, to be honest.

"Actually, George," she says quietly, "Can I speak to you about something?"

"Fire away."

She's fiddling about in her bag, and after a few tuts to herself, she pulls some folded, lined paper out of it. She tells me she's been getting these weird letters. Says they're from someone in the office.

"Let's see them, then," I say, putting my hand out to take them.

It's the weirdest thing, looking at letters you wrote but not in your own handwriting. The fact that I've kept it consistent when it was the most unnatural thing for me to do, is a stroke of genius.

I try so hard not to look suspect, but I manage to keep my expression at pure shock, and that's exactly where it will stay.

"What the fuck?!"

"I know," she says.

"I mean, who the hell would do this? It's sick. Have you reported it?"

"No. Not yet. I don't know what to do."

"What? Tell me you're joking?"

"I'm not joking. Honestly, I don't know whether I'm scared or not. I should be, shouldn't I? Maybe I'm as sick as the person sending them."

I tell her she is not sick. I tell her she's lovely, tell her that she should keep an eye on the content, and the frequency, of the notes. Tell her that, if it gets any worse, she must report it.

"I know," she says, "I have to go now. Norm will be going mad for his walk. Don't work too hard now, will you?"

"Yes, Miss."

LUCY ONIONS

27

I t's dark, so dark, and I think about not taking Norm out, but it's not fair on him. Anyway, a good walk will clear my head. Hopefully. I don't want to think about the letters. I don't want to think about work. I don't even want to think about George. I just want to walk.

Norm trots his small, but stocky, body a little in front of me. He's never strayed more than a few feet from my side, and tonight is no exception. If he does so happen to venture any further, he stops and looks at me as if to say, hurry up, I'm waiting.

One lap of the field, and one around the block, and we're back home. I unclip his lead, take his collar off, and give him a good scratch. He leans against my hand, clearly enjoying the fuss.

I warm up a bowl of tomato soup, pop some bread in the toaster, and because I'm feeling parched, I pour a large glass of water, down half of it in seconds. It refreshes me, quenches my raging thirst, but I want something stronger.

I grab a beer from the fridge and sit at the table with my bowl of hot, steaming soup in front of me. I'm a strong believer that food, whether it's breakfast, lunch or dinner, should be consumed whilst sitting at a table. It needs to be kept separate from slobbing out in front of the tv. That's what snacks are for.

28

I turn my computer off and feel happy with what I've achieved. Four manuscripts logged, read and processed in just under three hours. A record for me.

I tidy my desk, and take my dirty, coffee cup to the kitchen. I wash, rinse and dry it, put it back in its designated place. I'm a rare breed when it comes to office etiquette, in particular, keeping the kitchen tidy. Well, I'm a rare breed in this place at least. I mean, what does it take to just clear up after yourself? Hardly any time, or effort.

I know Iris sings from the same hymn sheet. She leaves no mess whatsoever in her wake.

We have cleaners, and maybe that's why the majority of people here think it's fine to leave all their filth for someone else to deal with – they don't get paid to be tidy. I dread to think what their houses look like.

I scan the office, check all computers are off, and windows are closed. I switch the lights off and lock the door behind me.

29

I wake with a start. I'm still on the sofa, my book on the floor where I must have dropped it. I don't know where the bookmark is, but it's definitely not inside. I turn my left wrist around and look at my watch. Twelve thirty. Shit. I really should be in bed.

Norm's snoring his head off, lying on the rug, and he looks so comfy that I almost don't want to wake him to come up to bed. But I can't sleep when he's not in the bedroom with me. I know he's a dog, I know I'm silly, but I find such comfort in knowing he's with me, in knowing he's not downstairs all on his own. I should leave him there. I've made a rod for my own back, I suppose. Actually, I don't care. He's my dog. I'll have him upstairs with me if I want to. It's not like there's anyone around to stop me.

If ever someone broke in, I'd only know when it's too late. Thank God for creaky floorboards. I can't bear to think what could happen to him if he accosted an intruder. I don't ever want to imagine. At least when he's with me, we can protect each other.

I stroke his back. He snores and splutters awake and looks at me with utter disdain. I open the back door, out on to the garden. He makes it quite clear that he will not be going out there, for his ritual pee. I wouldn't want to go out myself. Not in this. The wind is howling, the rain lashing. I gesture once more for him to go out, but no, he's not budging. Not an inch.

"Okay. Come on then," I tell him, and lock the door, shutting the world out.

He's at the bottom of the stairs, taking a few run-ups to gain the momentum needed to get him to the top. I don't move until he's firmly planted on the landing, and he looks down at me as much to say, Well, what are you waiting for?

I reach the top, giggle to myself as he ambles off to my room and jumps on my bed.

I brush my teeth, remove what little make up I still have on, and change into a fresh pair of pajamas.

I sink in to my bed, snuggle up to Norm and feel myself drift away.

30

She looks comfortable, peaceful, which is amazing considering Norm is taking up almost half of her bed.

It's freezing tonight.

What was I thinking?

I'm wet through, and my face, fingers and toes feel numb, nonexistent. It's all worth it though. So worth it.

I could honestly sit and watch her all night, but not tonight, not in this weather. There have been nights, particularly in the summer months, where I've not even gone home. I always keep a toothbrush, some toothpaste, a bottle of water, and some smells in my rucksack for such occasions. Always like to be prepared. Always like to be clean, no matter what I've been up to throughout the night.

As well as enjoying the view (I'm talking Iris, and some of the stunning dawns I've witnessed), I love hearing the birds and wildlife settle for the night, just to hear them start up again and wake the world. There's honestly nothing more beautiful than the sound of the dawn chorus, although Iris comes a very close second. I know the songs of the blackbirds in Iris's garden. I've come to recognise their calls to each other. It never gets old. Never gets boring.

The birds have gone quiet earlier tonight. Maybe it's their

warning. Maybe a storm is coming. Maybe it's time for me to say my silent goodbye and head home.

31

I switch on my computer and yawn. Have I actually had fourteen hours away from here? It doesn't feel like it. I could be worse off. I could be stuck in a dead-end, shitty excuse for a job. I should really think myself lucky.

Looks like George is running late. Strange. He's usually here before me.

I head to the kitchen, put my lunch in the fridge and wait in line for coffee. Adam and Lucas join the queue, behind me.

"Hey, Iris," Lucas says.

Adam doesn't speak, just cocks is head in silent greeting.

"Hi, guys," I respond.

"Feels like we're never away from here, doesn't it?" Adam says.

"I was just thinking exactly the same," I agree.

"Do you know where George is?" Lucas asks.

"Yeah," Adam adds, "it's weird not to see him first thing. I don't think he's phoned in sick. We would have heard by now. You know what it's like here for absences."

I nodded. I'd never worked anywhere where the management sarcastically announced absences over a speaker system, to the whole company, like it's some kind of competition. It's like high school, and houses, and scoring points, or losing them in this case. Touch wood, I have yet to phone in sick. I'm actually quite proud of that. I'd have to be really ill not to come in.

"Maybe one of us should phone him?" I say, wishing I'd thought of doing it earlier.

"We'll leave that to you, Iris," Adam smirks, and it puts me on edge, although I don't know why, "I think he'd rather hear your voice than one of ours. Don't say anything, but I think that he's got quite a soft spot for you."

I blush, losing the power of speech.

Lucas laughs.

Adam doesn't.

32

There's no way I'm going into work today. I rarely ever have time off work, but I feel like absolute death. I haven't slept a wink all night. Probably because of all the dithering, the high temperature and the insane amount of sweat I've produced. I need to phone in, but I need to get my head straight first.

My phone is vibrating next to me, on my bedside table. Seems the powers that be have beat me to it. I know I've got to answer, or it will just keep going on and on, send me round the bend.

Eyes closed, sensitive to the light that's filling my room (I really need to get some of those blackout blinds Adam keeps going on about), I jab my finger at the screen of my phone and hope for the best.

"Hi. George?" Iris's voice fills my head. I smile.

"Hi, Iris. Yes, it is he."

"I was just phoning to see if you were okay. Are you okay?"

I tell her that I'm not okay. That I haven't felt so not-okay in years. I'm not trying to get her sympathy. Actually, I guess I am. I don't tell her that though.

"Oh no. Well, get well soon, George. I'll let management

know you won't be in. Just make sure to phone in tomorrow though, okay?"

"Okay. You sound very official. Well done."

I hear her laugh.

I smile again, despite myself.

About four years ago, I broke my ankle in a stage dive that went awry. I didn't tell work that. I swore Adam and Lucas to secrecy, although they clearly thought it was hilarious.

Even though I had handed in a sick note which stated I would need six weeks off, I still had to phone in, every morning, to let them know I wouldn't be in. I mean, how stupid. I'm pretty sure they would have guessed I was absent when they noticed I wasn't there.

"I'm sorry," she says softly, "I just don't want you to get any grief."

"I know. Thank you, Iris."

"It's my pleasure. Actually, would you like me to bring you anything after work? Honey and lemon drink? Paracetamol?"

I tell her that that would be lovely, but that I'd hate for her to catch anything. She tells me not to be silly, and anyway, who am I to get in the way of a woman on a mission?

33

I haven't told Adam and Lucas I'm going to see George. I don't know why I feel like I should keep it from them, particularly Adam. I feel like it's my thing, not theirs. At the same time, it's got nothing to do with them. I made the phone call. I spoke to him. Shit, why am I feeling so defensive?

I log my computer off, happy that I have no outstanding work to catch up on. No doubt that will change by tomorrow.

I need to get some stuff for dinner tonight anyway. It's not like I'm making a special effort just for George.

I grab a basket, and pick up salad vegetables, tomatoes and spring onions, and a few, large jacket potatoes. Nothing beats a jacket when you're hungry, and there really is nothing more comforting when the weather's like this. Actually, a hearty, beef stew is even better.

I pick up what I need for that too. I'll do plenty, and if George is still ill tomorrow, I could take him a bowl after work.

I throw two packs of paracetamol, squeezy honey, some lemons and fresh ginger into the basket. I don't like those ready-made, packets of powdered cold and flu remedies.

Considering I only came in to get a few things, I'm leaving the shop laden with three, strong bags of shopping. It's a good job he doesn't live too far out of town. Oh yeah, I got his address at the same time as his number.

I'm beginning to worry about all these secrets I'm keeping, and the fact that I'm really not sure why they're actually *secrets*.

I turn on to his road, and now I'm outside his building. I press the buzzer for number three, and there's a click.

"Hello?" George's voice croaks through the speaker.

"It's Iris," I say, "I come bearing gifts."

34

She's standing in front of me, her arms weighed down with bags, and even though it's clear she's a little disheveled, she still looks bloody wonderful. I just stand and stare. I should ask her to come in. I will. I just need a second to take her all in.

"You going to invite me in, then?" she says, blowing her hair off her face.

I tell her I'm sorry, tell her I'm just not feeling myself. She nods sympathetically. I ask her in.

"So, I got you the essentials," she says, emptying the contents of one of the bags on to the dining table.

"You certainly have," I cough.

There's not a single energy drink in sight, no crap, no junk, just all good, natural remedies. I know she's not into ready-meals, or anything chemically enhanced. I've savoured the aromas coming from her home-cooked delights, from simple meals, and experimental efforts. I love watching her cook. She always looks like she's enjoying the whole process.

"How are you feeling now?" she asks.

I tell her I feel all the better for seeing her. She blushes, and once more, I am bowled over. I don't think I've ever known anyone as incredible as her. Yes, she's pretty. Not in a

I-won't-go-anywhere-without-a-full-face-of-make-up kind of way. She's naturally pretty, and that's great, but it's her personality that really does it for me. She's delicate, but in no way is she weak.

"I'll make you up a jug of honey, lemon and ginger. It's best to take it hot, or warm, and if you do want a little extra help, a drop of whiskey works a treat. Well, it does for me, anyway," she says.

I just want her to stop talking. I want her to stop flitting around. I want to grab her by those delicious hips, spin her around to face me, and kiss her because at this moment, it feels like my whole life depends on it. I don't think she'd be too thrilled with getting this shitty cold from me though.

"Thanks, Iris," I say, and make a mental note that I must be well when I see her again. I won't hold back next time.

35

Norm is doing his little happy-dance in front of me. I'll never tire of his warm, welcome home.

I throw my bags on the dining table, kick my shoes off and give him a big fuss. I tell him I can't do this all night, that I need to get dinner on. I stop tickling behind his ears and he walks off in one of his huffs.

I wash, prick, and salt, the biggest, baking potato of the lot and turn the oven to two hundred. I pour a glass of wine. I need it after my visit to George. Considering he's unwell, there was so much energy between us. So much chemistry. It took all of my strength not to kiss him. I think he felt the same too. It was a little awkward to say the least.

The red light on the oven pings off, notifying me it's up to temperature. I pop the potato on the middle shelf and set the timer to ninety minutes. It's the perfect time if you like a caramelised, crispy skin.

I slump on to the sofa and take an ample gulp of wine. I'm going to have to be careful because this is going down far too well.

36

I still feel like absolute shit and I know that all my body wants to do is stay in and rest, but I don't think I can go without seeing Iris for two days on the bounce. I know I saw her last night, but it just wasn't enough, and I know I'll start picking up the minute I see her face.

I pack my bag with today's essentials – pills, a pack of tissues, lozenges, and a couple of bottles of water. I can do this. I must. I need to.

The light dazzles me, hurts my eyes, as I step out onto the street. I put my sunglasses and find some relief behind tinted lenses.

I'm on my way to the café. Breakfast wasn't happening this morning. I just couldn't stomach anything so early. Buttered toast seems good right about now, and my stomach growls as I place my order. I eat way too quickly, both slices in less than a minute. Hello, indigestion.

I'm outside work. I take a deep breath and let it out long and slow. I've just got to open the door. How hard can it be?

Iris is surprised to see me. She says she didn't expect me in today at all. She asks me if I'm sure I should be here. She asks me if I'm okay. She tells me that if I need anything, I should let her know. If this was anyone else, asking me a million questions (okay, so that's a slight exaggeration!), I'd lose my shit. Completely. But it's Iris, and already, I'm starting to feel better. I'm not well, that's for sure, but she's exactly the person I need to see. That face could cheer up the most miserable person on the planet. I'd put money on it.

She hugs me. She actually hugs me, firmly, tightly. I'm pretty sure the whole office is witness to it. She's oblivious though and doesn't seem to care one bit as she walks back to her desk.

I shuffle past Adam and Lucas, and they both smile knowingly at me. I shake my head, denying their silent accusation, but as soon as I'm out of their sight, I smile.

There's hardly much of a pile on my desk, but I know it's going to take everything I have to get through it. I'm barely functioning as it is. Maybe my coming in today isn't one of my best ideas.

I pull both bottles of water from my bag and lay all the cold and flu paraphernalia out in a tidy pile next to my computer.

I boot it up, throw a couple of paracetamols in my mouth and wash them down with a slug of water.

I don't believe in God, but I pray today goes quickly.

37

There is absolutely no way he should be in work today. He looked so poorly last night. Still gorgeous though, nonetheless. I don't know what he must be thinking, coming in. He won't be thanked if he passes his germs on to everyone in the office.

He sits at his desk, looking utterly miserable, and all I want to do is give him another big hug.

I'm clock-watching, and it's something I hate doing. It never speeds up. In fact, I'd bet that time slows down the more I look at it.

Twelve-thirty rolls round, and I practically spring out of my chair. I pull my coat on, and without saying a word to anyone, I head out. I know exactly how I can cheer George up. At least, I think I do. A donut from the patisserie in town can turn any bad day into a good one. They're seriously the best I've ever tasted. So light. Delicious.

There's not much of a queue, which is a first because it's always packed at lunchtime. I pick out two, jam-filled donuts. I don't get all these fancy trimmings. Give me a classic any day of the week.

I eat my lunch in the park. It's cold, but it's dry, and the sun is shining. I don't know what George is doing for his lunch, and maybe I should just go back, eat my sandwiches at work, but the last thing I need is to be ill. Also, it's too nice a day to spend it completely indoors.

I lay my coat on the grass, and pull my lunch, and my book, out of my bag. George will just have to wait for his surprise, sweet treat.

38

Iris doesn't owe me a thing, but as I watch her leave, I can't help but feel hurt. She hasn't even looked at me, let alone ask if I want to join her. Not a word. If it was the other way around, I would ask her. Anyway, it's done. What can I do about it?

I stare at the can of tomato soup I've put, optimistically, on my desk. Why is it you want soup when you've got a cold? It doesn't make you feel any better, well, not in the long run anyway. In the short term though, that hot, steaming bowl of orange-red loveliness, is a comfort.

I'm still staring at it, and I honestly don't think I can bring myself to pull the lid off and pour the contents into a bowl. I don't think I can stomach it. It would be a total waste.

I get up from my chair slowly. I'd like to move a bit quicker because I'm desperate for a piss, but the mixture of being ill, and the loss of appetite, has made me feel dizzy.

The walk to the men's room is exhausting and painful. I feel like I'm scaling a fucking mountain. The floor comes up to meet me, and it takes every effort to stay upright. But I manage it, and finally push open the door.

Again, the effort to unzip my jeans and pull out my dick is tantamount to lifting a dead weight. I take hold of it with my left hand, and steady myself with my right. How come, even when you're desperate for a piss, it takes for-fucking-ever for the flow to come? It doesn't help that I'm feeling like death, but even so.

I yawn, a wide, loud, gaping yawn, but my breath catches in my throat and I break into a coughing fit. It stops almost as soon as it starts, and as I relax, the relief of imminent urination washes over me.

Feeling slightly more comfortable, I quickly wash my hands, and welcome the cold water that tumbles over them. I splash my face once, twice, and then one last time for good measure. I look at my reflection in the mirror, and it knows, just as well as I do, that I should not be here. I pull a green hand towel from the dispenser. Why the hell do they call them towels? They feel like they're only one thickness down from cardboard, and couldn't absorb air, let alone water. I may as well wipe a wet flannel over my face for all the good it does.

I stare at myself in the mirror again.

"Come on, you can do this," I whisper.

That's all the pep-talk I've got in me.

39

I can't see George anywhere, so I check with Adam and Lucas, and no, George hasn't gone home, although I really think that's the best place for him, right now. This must be torture for him, being in work when he's feeling like this.

I open my bag and pull out the brown paper one with the donut inside, put it on his desk. I hope it cheers him up, I really do. I head back to my desk, and as I sit down, I see him appear at the door, which he swings open with a heavy sigh. If anyone ever needed a hug so badly, it's George, now. I decide against acting upon my urge. I don't want to cause a scene.

He sits down and picks up the bag. Opens it. Looks inside, then at me, just as I smile at him and give him a little wave. Why didn't I just leave him a note? It would have been far less embarrassing.

40

Whatever feelings I had towards Iris at the start of lunch have now gone. The bad vibes have disappeared thanks to a single, jam-filled, fluffy treat. She has redeemed herself. She is forgiven.

I read far too much into her lunchtime excursion. Over analysing, as per usual.

When it comes to donuts, I know my thing, and that was just heavenly. Even through the blocked sinuses, I could taste. Even though I feel like shit, the sugar has perked me up. It's exactly what I needed.

I'll have to thank her later. As long as she doesn't mind me being too close.

41

Thank God for that. Time to call it a day.

I fight the urge to run up to him. Well, I fight it as much as I can. I head straight for him (without running), and he smiles as he sees me approaching.

I ask how he's feeling, and he tells me he's not well, but the donut has helped a little. I tell him he should really stay at home tomorrow if he still feels this bad. I tell him he needs to rest up and come back when he's one hundred percent. He shrugs his shoulders, promises me that he won't be setting foot in here if he doesn't feel any different.

I would love nothing more than to go back to his flat with him. Even if it's just to play Mother Hen. It's a natural thing to me, to want to look after people. Sometimes I wish I didn't care as much, but that's never going to change. Not now.

I give him a hug, let it linger a little, and say goodbye.

42

I don't follow straight after her, even though I can't wait to be back home, with the fire on full, and a hot toddy in my hand. I watch her though. Watch her exit the building. Watch her walk, her hips, and backside, swaying from side to side, across the asphalt, around the corner, and out of sight.

What I would do to her if I had the chance. No. I can't think like this. Not anymore. Everything has changed. I'm not the man I once was. Not the perverted weirdo I used to be. I've turned a corner. I really *like* her, and I know she likes me. That's what I need to hold on to. That she's not out of my league. That she's attainable. I don't have to stalk her from now on. There's no need to. She's happy to be seen with me. She's happy to be with me.

LUCY ONIONS

43

Norm doesn't come to greet me. I can't remember the last time that happened. He's asleep, and dreaming, on the rug. His legs are twitching, his tongue sticking out. He's whimpering. Must be a good one.

I don't know why I'm tip-toeing around him, trying to make as little noise as possible. He's not a child, he's a dog, but he's family all the same.

I don't usually drink straight after work, well, nothing alcoholic anyway. I usually make a cup of tea, or coffee. But I throw caution to the wind and pull a bottle of red from the rack. I unscrew the top, pour a large glass, and take it into the living room. I put the glass on the coffee table and fall backwards onto the sofa.

The first gulp of wine goes down well, and I sigh contentedly. I don't know why I need this. I just do. It's not been a stressful day, unless you class the strong feelings I have for George stressful. If I don't act on these feelings soon, they'll eat away at me. He's got to know I like him. I know he likes me. But we're both holding back. Maybe I need to make the first move?

I drain my glass, head to the kitchen, and pour another one. That's enough for tonight. No more.

I've got some leftover casserole that I took out of the freezer this morning. It's thawed properly, so I crack the lid open a little, and pop it in the microwave. I praise myself for always making extra. I'm in no mood to cook tonight.

As if on cue, Norm wakes up. He knows, instinctively, if there's any kind of food related activity going on. He stretches his limbs out, and paws at the rug, then bumbles over to me. I smile at him as he stops in his tracks, sniffing the air.

The microwave pings, and if his eyes weren't boring into my soul before, they certainly are now. I scoop casserole into two dishes now, giving Norm a smaller amount than me. I leave our food to cool a little. It's too hot to eat right now.

I pull my phone out of my bag. I had saved George's number the other day, and I stare at it on my phone screen. I know I've already used it to make contact with him, but that was purely on a professional basis.

Maybe I should just text him and be done with it. It's less formal than a phone call, and I can hide behind the words. Someone needs to get the ball rolling properly, and it looks like that someone is going to have to be me.

44

My phone vibrates in my pocket and scares the hell out of me. That's the problem with skulking about, on your own, in the dark, stalking. The phone screen lights up the room, hurting my eyes to look at it. There's no name, just a number, and the start of a message. It's from Iris. I swipe my index finger across the screen to read more.

Hi George, it's Iris. I really hope you don't mind, but I saved your number when I called you from the office the other day. I guess you could say I stole it from the system. I know, crazy right? I could have just asked you for it. I'd understand if you didn't want to text your nut-job, co-worker back.

Anyway, I just want you to know that I'm thinking of you, and I hope you feel better soon. I hope you enjoyed the donut, and if I haven't started alarm bells with my stalker-text, maybe we could go on a proper date? A donut date? Iris xxxxx

I feel a wide smile spread across my face. Is this for real? I know we've kind of hit it off already, but this, this is different. This is the next level. This is what I've wanted since I first ever laid eyes on her.

I'm not going to text back straight away. I'm going to wait

until I get back in the flat, read it again, and maybe once more. Just so it really sinks in. Then I'll get back to her.

45

I put Norm's bowl of casserole on the floor, and in an instant, his head is in it, and he's grunting like a pig.

I drag my bowl towards me and scoop up a spoonful. I put it in my mouth, staring dumbly at my phone screen. It's been ten minutes now, and still nothing. I know he's got the text, and I know he's read it, such is the wonder of modern technology.

Would I have answered a text from him if I hadn't given him my number? I think I would. I'm sure I would. Maybe he doesn't feel anything for me. Either way, he needs to respond. At least then I'll know where I stand.

LUCY ONIONS

46

I grab a beer from the fridge and pop the cap, leaving it to lie exactly where it falls.

The voice in my head tells me to think about this one, tells me not to be desperate. I nod to myself, take a gulp of the cold, refreshing liquid and start to tap out my reply.

Hi, Iris. It's great to hear from you even if you did steal my number to do it! Xx Thank you for today. I enjoyed my donut very much. It made a dull day seem a little brighter. A donut date, eh? Sounds great. Maybe if we go at the weekend, we can go to the pub afterwards? Really make a night of it?

I stop and look at what I've just typed. Shit. It sounds a bit needy. Does it? I'm not exactly well practiced in communicating with the opposite sex, let alone arranging dates with them. I'm not going to change it though, not now. It's what I want to say, what I've wanted to say for such a long time, albeit without mention of donuts. I'm going to be me. No acting.

47

I almost jump out of my skin as my phone buzzes, its screen lighting up. I see the notification, including the first couple of lines of a text message. It's from George. My stomach is doing somersaults, and even though I can't wait to open the text and read it, my heart feels like it's going to burst out of my chest. I'm not a teenager anymore, I'm a grown-bloody-woman. What the hell is wrong with me?

With a deep breath, I swipe my finger from left to right, over the mini message. I smile as I see that it's a decent length, but then, compared to the ones I get from my Mum, I'd class a couple of sentences an essay.

I take two, large gulps of my wine, which results in an empty glass, and the courage required to read it.

My mouth breaks into the biggest smile. My face hurts from it.

I read the text once more, and don't stop myself breaking into giggles. I feel like I'm back in school, reading the note that Jack Devon dropped into my bag. I'll still never know how he managed to do that without me seeing, but he did. I'm so glad he did. I'll never, ever forget that day, how his note made me feel. And now, it's like I'm stood back in that corridor, and everything is perfect.

Me and Jack, well, we probably shouldn't ever have dated. Should never have been girlfriend and boyfriend. We were such good friends, even though I was a geek and he was far too popular with the girls. He was in the *in* crowd, a crowd I never stood a chance of getting in to. I didn't want to be part of it, to be honest, and that was the reason it didn't work out with him, but that note meant the world to me.

What do I text back? I've got to be careful here. Whatever I type back could sound desperate, but I can't not reply, that would just be plain rude.

My index finger hovers over the touchscreen keypad, and I begin.

Donuts and pub? Sounds great. I look forward to it. Now, go rest, and I'll see you when I see you. Goodnight, George. Iris xxx

48

My eyes flicker open, and I realise I'm on the sofa. Norm's snoring (no surprise there). That's probably what's made me wake up. It's a blessing in disguise really because I would have, no doubt, been down here until morning.

I sit up and carefully move my legs from around him. He chunters, huffs and puffs, but he doesn't wake. It would take a world war, or a monumental natural disaster to shock him awake. We don't have a hope in hell if someone were to break in. Or maybe he would surprise me, and actually *protect* me. Stranger things have happened.

I stretch, stand up, and take my empty glass and bowl into the kitchen. I draw the blinds, lock out the darkness, and walk back to the living room. I notice a square piece of white paper on the rug, right in front of the French doors. I pick it up.

It's square because it's been folded. It wasn't there before I dozed off. I check the French doors and feel my stomach drop. They're unlocked. Shit. I could have sworn I locked them once Norm had come back inside.

Paper in hand, I check my front door. It's locked. Thank God for that.

It's so unlike me to forget about locking up. The front

door is locked the second I get in from work. I know I'm in the house, but I do it to feel safe, to protect us. When I go to bed, I check, and check again, all windows and doors. This really is very unusual, and it's made me feel nauseous.

I sit down, and try to calm myself, but turning the folded-up paper over, and over, in my hands isn't helping matters. I thought this had stopped.

Iris,

Sorry for my lack in correspondence. I've been so tired and a little under the weather. That's no excuse though, is it? It was just a lapse, a little blip. I'm feeling more like my usual self now though, and I'm happy to say that normal service has most definitely resumed, hence this letter.

I've not stopped thinking of you, Iris. I've had some extra time on my hands, and what better way to fill it.

I don't know what I would do if I hadn't got you. You are everything to me. Don't ever leave me, Iris. I beg you. Please. I can't imagine my life without you in it. I hope you feel the same. I've never actually asked you what you feel about me, have I? I will. One day. That's a promise.

Anyway, you take care now. Oh, and remember, I'm always watching you, Iris. I've got your back.

All my love, forever.

49

I watch her read the note, and then, even though I've just watched her do it, she checks the French doors. She looks out into the garden. I'm hiding, of course. She won't catch so much as a glimpse of me, but I'm tempted. Tempted to jump out and surprise her. And now I'm thinking how absolutely fucking ridiculous that would be.

LUCY ONIONS

50

I want to sleep. Really want to. But I'm freaked out.

I thought all this had stopped. It's not as if the note could have just been pushed under the doors. Whoever has left it, has opened them. Did they know I'd left it unlocked? Or did they just take a punt? Hope for the best? Either way, this *stalker* (yes, that's what this is. I have a stalker) has been in my garden. Fuck. What if they're still here?

LUCY ONIONS

51

My alarm wakes me with a start, my head feels like it's going to shatter into a million little pieces, and I'm burning up.

I know I shouldn't even have contemplated going to check in on Iris. I could have delivered the note once I'm feeling better. Now I feel even worse, and I know I won't be making it into work.

I reset my alarm, allowing another hour for sleep. Then I'll make the dreaded phone call.

LUCY ONIONS

52

I wake up, groggy. That's what getting only a few hours sleep does to you. It was twenty-past-three when I last glanced at my alarm clock. Oh well, four hours then. Doesn't feel like it.

Norm doesn't budge an inch as I heave myself out of bed. I'm so tempted to phone in sick. So, so tempted.

The kitchen feels freezing, colder than usual. I put it down to tiredness and grab my tin of ground coffee from the cupboard. My autopilot kicks in, and before I know it, I've started the percolator off. I suppose the routine of it all is second nature. No real thought involved. I just need this drink and I'll feel right in no time.

I pop some bread in the toaster, and stand, watching, waiting, sipping at my too hot, caffeine laden drink. I'm not hungry, not really, but I have to eat. I can't function properly on an empty stomach. The only reason I'm having toast is because my banana stock seems to have depleted overnight.

The slices of toast jump out of their hot slots, and I pick them out, juggling them before practically throwing them onto a plate. I spread salted butter on both slices and sigh as I watch it melt. Now I'm hungry. I almost dribble. I take a bite of one slice. It's so good.

I finish my breakfast, fill Norm's water bowl, and pour some complete, dry mix into his food bowl. He shoves his head in it the minute I step away. Greedy dog.

I wash quickly, put on a little tinted moisturizer, the bare minimum of eyeshadow, and mascara. I finish with a touch of tinted lip balm.

I'm not even going to attempt trying to find a fresh outfit, can't be bothered to rifle through my wardrobe. There's nothing wrong with what I wore yesterday. It'll do.

Norm's sitting right in front of the front door. It's the same every morning. I'm sure he does it on purpose, trying to make me feel guilty. He knows exactly what he's doing.

He gives me the eyes, and I kiss him on the head. His tail starts to wag, and I say goodbye.

53

The text reads:

Hi, George. How are you? Obviously, you're not here, so I'm guessing you're not feeling great. Let me know if you need anything. Iris xxx

What I need is to hurry the fuck up and get better. It's killing me, not seeing her. Last night really wasn't my greatest idea. If I'd have just stayed in, maybe I'd be well enough to actually drag my backside into work, and then I'd be able to get my fix.

Maybe I need therapy. I know what I'm doing is wrong and if she ever finds out it's me that's stalking her, that's it. It will be all over, and it will all by my fault.

I text her back, thank her, tell her I'll be back as soon as I can.

Well, just make sure you're back to normal before you do. It's crazy here today. Just stay away as long as you need to. Iris xxx

I don't want to though. I mean, work, yes, I'd happily stay away. I get sick pay. It's not an issue. The simple fact is, I don't want to stay away from her.

I pop two paracetamols in my mouth and swallow them down with a gulp of water. I just need to keep taking the pills and rest up. I need to get better. I need to see her.

LUCY ONIONS

54

I keep looking over at George's desk. I can't help myself. What do I think is going to happen if I keep staring at his swivel chair? Will he magically appear? This is stupid, really silly. I'm missing him.

I tear my eyes away and switch my focus to the pile of submissions in front of me. This is what I need, to read, to banish all thoughts of George from my mind.

I read the synopsis page of the first submission on the pile. Without even having to start on the three-chapter excerpt, I just know this is erotic fiction. And, if I'm correct, not even half decent. I flick the page over and start to read. Within the first few paragraphs, my assumption is confirmed. If this is how it starts, then I would seriously advise the author to go to a creative writing class, and re-educate themselves on structure, dialogue, and most importantly, plot.

I just can't get past the first page. I want to try, I really do, but it's shocking. I put it to one side and hope to God the next one will be better.

I finish reading the last submission, and as I look up, I realise the office is empty. I never heard anyone leave, probably because I've been totally engrossed in what I've just read. I'm definitely putting this one in the *call back* pile.

The door swings open, and in comes the cleaner, dragging a vacuum with a happy little face on it, behind him. I've never seen our cleaner without his utility belt, heavy with an array of cleaning products and clothes. I like to imagine that he whips his anti-bacterial spray out, as a cowboy would do his pistol. He amazes, and amuses me, in equal measure.

Fred shouts over to me, asks why I'm still here. Tells me I ought to stop staying over at work because no one thanks you for it.

I smile and tell him I'm finished.

"That's what you always say, Iris," he laughs, looks down at the waste paper bin to his left, and starts to whistle.

I chuckle to myself. Fred is one of those people who, no matter what you're feeling, will always bring a smile to your face. He's never unhappy, and if he is, you would never know. He's caring, kind, polite and respectful. A proper gentleman.

I glance over to that sorry excuse of erotic fiction I tossed to one side earlier. *No, don't even think about it*, I tell myself. But I find I'm leaning across my desk, being drawn to it. *Don't you even dare!* My hand hovers over it. *No! No, no, no!*

And that's it. It's in my hand, and I quickly shove it in my bag, hoping Fred's so lost in his own little world that he doesn't notice. I shake my head, embarrassed at myself.

I pour myself a large Cabernet Sauvignon, pull the three chapters of filth from my bag, and sink into my armchair. I can't believe I'm about to do this, can't believe I'm going to give it the time of day. I take a large, steadying gulp, and inhale deeply.

I finish the glass by the second chapter. Whether it's to do with the alcohol, or what I've read, maybe it's both, I'm not sure, but my cheeks start to burn hot.

55

I'm the first in. I knew I would be. I had to be.

It's eight am, and there's not another soul in sight. I tiptoe to Iris's workstation and drop the note on her desk. I sneak away, giggling like a naughty school boy who's left a stink bomb for someone to find.

I feel better. Not the best I've felt by any means, but better. And anyway, even if I still felt like absolute shit, I'd be in. I'd made my mind up that I was coming into work today, without fail.

The door opens, and in walks Iris. Eight thirty on the dot. She walks straight past my desk, oblivious to my presence, lost in whatever music is playing through her earphones.

I watch her get her workspace in order, and giggle as she starts singing along to her music. She's loud enough that I can hear she's listening to Whatever Gets You Through the Night by John Lennon. I'd know the track anywhere.

She doesn't start all out dancing, but she's shimmying and swaying, and then suddenly, she stops, spots me spying on her. Her cheeks flush red, and she rips the earphones out of her ears.

"You saw all of that, didn't you?" she asks, eyes closed.

"Yup," I nod.

She laughs, clearly embarrassed.
"Someone shoot me now!"

56

I*ris,*

I need to know if I'm doing the right thing. Do you even like getting my letters anymore? I have to know. I put so much of myself into them. There's nothing off-the-cuff about what I write to you. I put a lot of time, and effort in. Do you see that? Can you read it in my writing?

I can't expect you to understand me. How could you understand someone you've never even met? That's what you're asking yourself, isn't it? But you have, Iris. You've met me. You know me. I want you to know me better. I want you to know me as much as I know you. It's why I write these letters.

Do you want to know me? To see who I really am? Or are you happy to fantasise? Do you like the mystery of it all?

I need to know.

I have to know.

From the day I first saw you' I've been hooked. You're like a drug. I can't get enough of you.

You are the last thing I think about before I close my eyes, and the first thing I think about when I open them.

You just don't know what you do to me.

I love you, Iris.

LUCY ONIONS

57

I ris walks towards me. I look at the piece of folded paper in her hand before she quickly puts it in her trouser pocket.

"Hey, George," she says, clearly flustered, "it's good to see you. Are you feeling better?"

"Much better, thanks. You okay?"

"Oh, yeah. Fine, thanks," she says, but there's a but, "Well, actually, I don't know if I am."

"How do you mean?" I ask her, desperately trying to keep my face straight.

She takes the note, my note, out of her pocket.

"This," she says, handing it to me.

Of course, I don't need to read it, but I put on a good performance of doing so.

"Another one?" I ask.

She nods.

"When did you get it?" I ask, feeling excitement starting to flow through me. I like this game.

"Last night. It was on the floor by the French doors in my living room. I'd been asleep, and when I woke up, there was a letter, just like this."

"Was there any sign of a break in?"

She shakes her head.

"I left the doors unlocked," she says, "stupid, right? Anything could have happened."

I get up from my chair, gesture for her to sit down on it. I pull up a spare one and sit next to her. It's probably not the best thing to do, but I put my arm around her shoulders. I almost expect her to back away, but she seems to relax under my touch. I rub the top of her arm.

"Hey, it's okay," I say.

"Is it? I don't know what to do. My head is telling me to report this to the police, but what could they actually do, George?"

"I'm honestly not sure, Iris. I don't know how they deal with this kind of thing. At the moment, it's just letters, isn't it? Hopefully this will be as bad as it gets."

"Yeah, I hope so too."

"But if it makes you feel any better, just notify them. Let them know what's going on. They might give you a crime number or something, then if it does escalate for any reason, they have the case on file."

She smiles and puts her head on my shoulder. Her hair smells incredible, and it takes everything I have to stop myself from sticking my face in it, so as I can breathe it all in.

"You'll let me know if you get any more?"

"Yes," she nods, softly rubbing her cheek up and down on my shoulder. I wonder if she realises she's doing it.

"Oh, sorry," she says, sitting up straight.

"For what?"

Her cheeks turn red.

"George?" she says, just about managing to look me in the eye, "seeing as it's Friday, how about we go out tonight?"

"What, for our donuts and beer?"

"Uh huh!"

This is it. It's happening.

"Why the hell not!"

58

The donuts, as always, are piping hot, utterly delicious, but the beer, the beer is even better. Not so much the taste, although it's going down far too easily, but the fact that I'm sitting here, across from George, drinking, well, I haven't felt this happy in so long. I need this. These letters are really starting to trouble me. The more I think about them, the more I seem to get them. I thought they weren't getting to me too much, but they are. I'm glad I've been able to tell someone about them, even more glad that George is the person I've confided in.

"I'm going to the bar," he says, snapping me out of my trance, "same again?"

I nod, and watch, mesmerised as he walks away. It's hard not to notice how good his backside looks in those jeans, and the way his biceps, which are just the right size, flex and tighten as he leans against the bar.

It's not packed in here tonight, but it's busy enough to warrant more than two members of serving staff. George lets out a short, sharp whistle, and waves a twenty-pound note, trying to catch the eye of a bartender. I usually find this behaviour rude, but it doesn't seem that way with George. There's no malice in his actions. As if the bartender has picked up the smell, he looks straight at George, smiles, and starts to serve.

"Here you go," George says, clearing a bubbly white strip of beer froth from his top lip with his tongue.

I thank him, taking a deep gulp from my bottle.

"This is nice," he says.

I study my drink, take another mouthful, and agree with him. It really is a nice drop. Nutty and rich, refreshing.

"Not the beer, silly," he laughs, "the company. This. It's just really nice to be here with you."

I couldn't agree more.

"That's me done," I tell George. I'm starting to feel a little giddy, "I know my limit."

"I'll walk you home," he offers. I'm not about to refuse.

He necks what's left of his beer, stands up, walks around the table to me, and offers me his arm.

Who said chivalry is dead?

59

Iris is so different outside of work. I'd got just the smallest taste of that after the gig the other night. Okay, she was nervous. So was I. But tonight, whatever awkwardness we both felt towards each other, has disappeared.

Maybe it's because she told me about the letters? Maybe she just needed to get it all off her chest? The fact that she trusts me enough to tell me, blows me away. It makes me so happy. I know I've said it before, but maybe I should really think about stopping. I mean it this time.

"Want to come in?" she suddenly asks me. I look up and realise we're outside her house. I look at her, my eyes searching hers.

"Do you want me to?"

She nods at me. Something in her eyes tells me all I need to know.

She asks me if I want a drink. Coffee? Tea? Something stronger? I ask her if she has beer. She only has wine, red wine. I tell her that that'll do. She tells me to make myself at home, so I head into the living room, and drop on to her sofa. I feel comfortable, feel that this was all meant to happen, in this way, now.

She practically floats into the room with two glasses of

wine, and places them on coasters on the coffee table. She sits down beside me.

"I've really enjoyed it tonight," she says, taking a sip from her glass. She's not drunk, but she has a certain flush to her cheeks, and it might just be me mishearing, but her words seem slightly slurred.

"It's not over yet," I tell her.

She smiles widely.

"Thanks for coming back," she says, "I'm really glad you're here."

"It's a pleasure," I say, "thanks for asking me. I'm glad I'm here too."

She blushes, looks at her watch.

"Oh my God, is that the time?"

I look at mine. It's eleven forty-five and I really don't know where the time has gone. I nod at her, silently confirming that it is, indeed, late.

"I'll just drink this then I'll go," I stand up, swallowing half a glass of wine in one go.

Iris grabs my arm.

"No, you don't have to," she says, and I see that look in her eyes again.

I tell her it's okay. Tell her we've both had a drink, that we can do this again soon.

"No," she insists, "please stay."

She pulls gently at my arm and I sit back down beside her.

She finishes her wine quickly, winces as she downs the last drop.

The atmosphere in the room has changed. It's intense, filled with anticipation. I swear I can hear both of our hearts beating.

And then, she gulps. I mean really gulps. She turns to me, and it's hard not to notice the fact that she's shaking. Only a little, but enough to see that she's nervous. I open my mouth to ask her if she's okay, but the words never leave.

60

I pull out of the kiss, shocked at my actions. His face is a picture, and I can't help but smile. I apologise for my outburst.

"What for?" he asks.

He's right. What for? Why should I say sorry when I don't really mean it? It's silly. I've wanted to kiss him for so long. I've thought of nothing much else to be honest. It was always going to happen. This kiss was inevitable.

"Iris?" he asks quietly.

"Yes?"

"You okay?"

I tell him I'm fine. Because I am. More than fine.

He smiles sweetly, and we both look at our feet. The atmosphere is intense. Quiet enough to hear a pin drop. Fully charged.

I tell him I'm tired, that I'm ready for bed. I make eyes at him, flirting as best I can, hoping he'll get the hint.

He rearranges the cushions on the sofa.

"I'm okay down here," he says, and although I'm a little disappointed that he won't be joining me, I'm happy that the night has ended like this.

61

The unmistakable smell of frying bacon fills my nostrils. I can hear Iris pottering around in the kitchen even though I never heard her come downstairs. I get up and head towards her.

"Mm, something smells good," I say.

"Hope you like bacon! Oh shit, do you? I mean, do you eat meat? I should have checked with you first."

I tell her to relax, tell her that, yes, I do eat meat and that bacon is my weakness. She sighs and smiles.

"That's good then. I think I've cooked enough to feed a small army."

She's not wrong. There's already a pile of well-cooked rashers on a plate beside the oven hob.

"I think you can stop cooking now," I laugh. She laughs too.

There are two glasses of orange juice on the table, and the smell of freshly brewed coffee fills the air around me.

All of this, sitting here watching Iris flit about, seeing her smiling, and hearing her humming along to a tune I cannot hear, as she's preparing breakfast, all seems so natural. I feel like I'm meant to be here. That we're meant to be.

She places a mug of coffee next to my orange juice,

closely followed by a plate piled with bacon, scrambled eggs, grilled tomato and sautéed mushrooms. I'm not going to tell her I don't think I'll eat it all, that there's far too much for me. That's just rude.

She's sitting to the side of me now, and even if I wasn't looking at her, I'd be able to feel those gorgeous eyes boring into the side of my head. I take it that she wants me to eat so I scoop some of the egg up. It's delicious. I don't know what she's done to make it taste so good, but it's definitely the best I've ever had.

"Try the bacon," she commands with a smile.

Again, it's delicious. I had no doubt of that. I tell her it's all excellent.

"Really?" she asks, blushing.

"Really."

"The meat and eggs are free range, thanks to my Aunt" she says, "and the mushrooms and tomatoes are organic. I grow those myself. I'll show you my greenhouse later, if you like?""

"I'd love that," I say, even though I've spent a great deal of my time hanging round next to it.

She smiles at me. I return the gesture and tuck back in.

62

He's drying the plates with enthusiasm. Who does that? Who actually enjoys drying, or indeed, washing plates? We get through it in half the time it usually takes me. He didn't need to help. I didn't ask him to help. But I'm glad all the same.

"Do you fancy doing something today?" he asks, dropping the tea towel over a drawer handle.

I tell him that that would be lovely, ask him if he has anything particular in mind.

"Not really," he says, "we'll just see what happens."

I tell him that that sounds like a plan.

"I need to go home and change first, though."

"That's okay," I say, "I need to get ready too."

He grabs his coat, kisses my cheek. What a gentleman! I steal a proper kiss, and he does nothing to stop me.

LUCY ONIONS

63

She looks amazing. Not overdressed, not underdressed. Perfect. Simple. Stunning yet understated.

"Hey," she says, sounding nervous. I don't know why she would be, but then again, our relationship has turned a corner. We've moved forward. I ask her if she's okay. She nods, tells me she's fine.

There's not a great deal to do in this town other than go shopping, take a walk in the park, or go to the pub. The way she's dressed though, suggests she has no interest in the first two options.

"Pub?" she asks, reading my mind.

She sits next to me on the Chesterfield. I ask her what she would like to drink.

"I'll have a cider, please," she says, adjusting herself. I stand up and head to the bar.

I pull out my wallet from my inside pocket, and very nearly pull the letter out with it. I shove it back in quickly and make a mental note to keep it safe. She'll get it, but not just yet.

I know, I know. I'm stupid. I should stop. But I can't help it. I keep telling myself, this will be the last one, but it never is. If I stop the letters, that's a huge part of my life gone. I know I don't need to write them any longer. I don't need to sneak around, but I'm addicted. Totally addicted.

64

I've had four ciders, and I can feel the effect they're having on me already. I'm not drunk, I'm just right.

The conversation has flowed easily, and even though the pub is busy and bustling with life, I feel like we're the only people in here.

"Right, I can't hold it in any longer," he says, getting up from the sofa, "I'm bursting for a piss."

I laugh, too loudly.

I'm giddy with excitement, and although the alcohol has helped in some way, it's not entirely down to that.

I try to drag my eyes away as he walks towards me, but it's impossible. He commands attention without even trying. There's this calm, cool swagger about him. I can see the other girls scattered around the bar; I can see how they're breaking conversations to look at him. It's getting my back up and I feel stupid for feeling that way because it's not them he's looking at. It's me.

65

I ris has matched me pint for pint. How she doesn't need to evacuate her bladder by now is beyond me. I couldn't hold it any longer. I thought I was going to explode and drown in a tsunami of my own piss.

Iris is blushing, smiling. It's infectious, and even though the pub is busy, there's only one person I'm looking at.

I didn't think anyone could look so pure. I know that sounds sickly sweet, soppy, but it's the truth. It's like she's some kind of divine being. Nothing and no one could ruin her. She's above all of it, all of us.

Maybe it's the drink talking, but I honestly have never felt this way about anyone. Ever.

"Do you want another drink?" she slurs, ever so slightly.

"Do you?"

She nods, giggles at some silent joke. I hope the joke isn't on me.

I think it's about time we leave. That extra drink turned into three and even though we're not falling about all over the place, it's time to quit while we're ahead.

"Do you want to come back to ours?" I ask her, hoping

that Adam and Lucas are off out somewhere.

"I'd like that," she giggles, swinging my arm playfully.

"As long as you don't mind Adam and Lucas being around?"

"Ah, no wonder you're so close," Iris says, "you've got brilliant chemistry on stage. I really dig that."

Dig? Seriously? She is so fucking cute.

"So you don't mind?"

"Of course not. The more the merrier."

66

George's hand envelopes mine. It's warm, not clammy. It's the perfect fit. I love how it feels. Maybe it's the drink talking. If it is, I don't care, but I feel safe. His hand, surrounding mine, feels as much metaphorical as it does physical. He's got me. He's not letting go.

We're walking in complete silence, and that's fine. Sometimes, words just ruin things.

I steal glances at his face on our journey to his place. I don't think he's noticing until his perfect, side profile, breaks into a smile.

"What?" he says, cheeks flushing red.

"Nothing."

67

She needs to stop. Seriously. I don't think she realises what she's doing to me. The stuff that's going around in my head right now, well, it's not something I could ever say out loud to her. My cheeks are heating up just thinking about it.

I fumble for my keys and hear Iris take a deep breath. She's not nervous, is she?

"You okay?" I ask her, finally sliding the key into the lock.

"Yes, I'm fine."

I'm sure I hear her gulp.

"Guys, you home?" I call out and hope there's no answer.

I'm nervous and I don't know why. Adam and Lucas are my best friends and it's not like they don't already know Iris. We work with each other for fucks sake. It's Adam that's the main issue, if there actually is one. I can't work him out. No, I can. I think. He's the green-eyed monster personified. Admittedly, there's a little bit of history between us. I think he gets jealous of anyone I bring home. Not that there have been many. Iris is only the third, proper girlfriend I've ever had. I've had a few one-night-stands that amounted to no more than that. He didn't exactly jump for joy when I bought them back either.

What happened between us was brief, and although it wasn't exactly unpleasant, it was a mistake. A silly, drunken mistake. He said as much himself. And my God, does he know how to lord it about! There's flirting and then there's what Adam does. He's not exactly been hard done by in the love-interest department. For each of my few girlfriends, he's had triple the number of boyfriends, if not more

"Yeah," I hear my best friends mumble, and even though my heart drops a little, I slap on a smile and gesture for Iris to go in ahead of me.

68

Adam and Lucas are sitting next to one another on the sofa, game console controllers hanging limp in their hands. We've obviously interrupted their progress in whatever game they are playing, but Adam's face seems the sourer of the two.

I've never understood it myself, how people can get so caught up in a video game, but then I've never really played any. I'd much rather sit and read a book or watch a good film.

"Hi, guys," I say, feeling nervous. I don't know why I should feel this way. I work with them, but I can't help it. And I don't think Adam's look of disdain is entirely to do with the game he's just had to pause prematurely.

"Hi, Iris," Lucas replies, holding his hand up, half waving.

Adam smiles at me. Is it a smile though? I can't tell. Whatever it is, is making me feel even more uncomfortable. Lucas elbows his friend in the side, mumbles something I can't hear.

I take that as my cue, and head after George. Anything to squirm my way out of whatever that atmosphere was.

"You okay," George says, busy getting beer out of the fridge.

I tell him I am. I'm a good liar.

"You okay?" I ask back because it's not exactly hard to pick up on the sense of unease hanging over him either.

"Yeah, I'm cool," he says and hands me a beer. I don't need to drink any more, but I don't refuse his offer. He gets two more from the fridge without asking his friends if they want one.

"Come through," he says after a long, deep swig of beer, closely followed by a burp.

I follow him back through to the living room and he offers me the last seat, an armchair that looks like it's seen a lot of life. He perches himself on the arm of it, leaning into me. His puts his arm around my shoulders, resting his beer on his left thigh.

You could cut the atmosphere with a knife right now. Lucas looks like he wants to crawl up his own arse and it seems to me that Adam knows exactly what he's doing. He knows he's the one causing this air of uncertainty. No one really knows what to say to drag us out of this fog.

And then.

"What is it tonight, then?" George says, breaking the heavy silence.

Adam totally ignores him, but Lucas looks and sounds relieved as he explains exactly how far into the level of the game they've been playing.

And then, silence. Again.

"Anyway, can we get on?" Adam finally speaks.

"Yeah, 'course," George nods.

"Erm, on our own?" Adam adds.

Lucas looks down at his hands, shakes his head.

"Okay," George answers, baffled, "Come on, Iris."

He takes my hand, helping me up from the depths of the saggy, soft chair.

He shuts his bedroom door behind us, locking out the awkwardness that followed us up the stairs.

"Jeez, what was all that about?" I ask, relieved.

"Long fucking story and one for another time."

I decide it's best not to press any further.

69

I could kill Adam. Right now. Seriously. I could happily go down there, put my hands round his throat and... No, I couldn't. Who am I kidding? I'd never hurt him, no matter how much he winds me up. But what the fuck is he playing at? I hate mind games and he's proving to be the master of them at the moment. I'm a grown man, but I feel like a child. The last person to confine me to my room was my mother. Why am I doing as he says? We all pay rent, not just him. I should go down there and have it out with him. And I would if Iris wasn't here. She doesn't need this aggro. I asked her back here and I want her to feel comfortable, even if it does mean I have to sneak her away.

She's looking around my room, flicking through books, CDs and records, totally lost in her own little world, making all the right sounds.

"Oh my God," she practically squeals with delight, "I thought it was only me who liked these guys! I've yet to find anyone who loves them as much as me."

"You have now," I say, proudly.

"So, spit it. What's your favourite song?" she asks, waving Moist's first album, Silver, at me.

"Oh, now that's not fair."

"Come on," she giggles and swigs at her bottle.

"Could you choose a favourite?"

"No. But that's not the point. I'm asking you, not the other way around."

I tell her, metaphorical gun to my head, that it has to be Push, but then, I imagine most fans of the band would say that too.

"Mine too," she says, "It's one of my most listened to songs ever. I discovered them quite late on, really, but better late than never, I guess."

"Same here," I agree with her, "and this is why we're meant to be together."

Shit.

Did I just say that out loud?

Way to go, George.

Silence.

Again.

"Sorry," I say, wishing there was a nice, dark corner for me to creep in to, "I didn't mean. You know. Damn it."

"It's fine. Don't worry. I get what you mean."

"You do?"

"I do."

We're chilling out on my bed and I feel like a teenager again. Of my last three girlfriends, there was only one I truly loved – the last one. I idolised her. I thought we'd be together forever. Yes, I know that sounds ridiculously cliché but it's true. She did a good job on me in the end, but whilst we were together, I felt the world revolved around the two of us. Doing this with Iris, drinking beer, listening to records, relaxing, well it's déjà vu. And even though this isn't our first date, it feels like it is. Fresh. New.

She's trying so hard to stay awake, fighting against her drooping eyelids. And then her eyes roll backwards in their sockets, only briefly, accompanied by her head lolling back and snapping forward again.

"I'm sorry," she says, more to herself than me, "I don't know why I'm so tired. I'm just going to put my head here and close my eyes. You don't mind, do you?"

She nuzzles her head into the crook of my neck, and no, I don't mind at all.

70

My mouth feels like a desert. If I would have remembered to grab a glass of water before I dropped off into one of the deepest sleeps I've ever had, it would have felt a little less dry.

I wasn't planning on staying over. If I was, I would have bought my pyjamas, toothpaste, you know, all the essentials you generally need if you're sleeping over. God, that sounds like I'm about twelve.

I smack my lips together, willing saliva to moisten my mouth. Then, there's that sudden realisation – my breath stinks. I can still taste the alcohol consumed last night and not much else to be honest.

I can't stay here, smelling like this. It's embarrassing.

I peel myself off George and wonder how in the hell either of us have managed to sleep. I sniff my armpits as quietly as it's possible to do such a thing and nod. Not bad. I tread softly from the room and head towards what I hope is the bathroom. My bladder feels like it's going to erupt.

I inch open the door and to my relief, it's the room I need. Considering three men use it, it's surprisingly clean and uncluttered. Minimal.

I flinch a little as my behind hits the toilet seat. It's cold, refreshingly so. It starts me off and I feel like this may be the longest pee ever. I smile in relief.

I know I shouldn't, but I've spotted an electric toothbrush and three detachable heads and although it's not at all hygienic, I seriously need to brush my teeth. My need far outweighs any fear of what I could possibly catch. It's fine. No worries.

Each brush head has a different coloured ring around it and I wonder what George's colour is. I sing eenie-meenie-minie-mo in my head and land on yellow. Here goes.

Of course, there's no hiding the sound of an electric toothbrush at work, but because I can't hear a single peep out of Adam, George and Lucas, I hope their sleeping is deep enough to cancel out the steady buzzing it's about to make.

Instant refreshment hits me, and I run my tongue over my teeth and mouth. I'm human again. I rub the bar of soap between my hands, watching as the froth grows. It's mesmerising. I wash and rinse my face, and with eyes firmly closed, feel about for a towel. My stomach drops when I realise one is being held out to me.

"Feeling better now?"

71

Iris appears at the door. Her face is pale, devoid of colour. She looks like she's seen a ghost. I hope she hasn't. I'm not good with shit like that.

"You okay?" I ask.

"Yeah. Yeah, of course."

The look in her eyes is telling me a completely different story.

"Sure?"

"Yes. Sure."

There's a saying that you can't bullshit a bullshitter. I know she's lying to me, but I'm not going to push any more. I've got the strongest feeling that this is about Adam. He wasn't exactly welcoming to Iris last night. I wonder if he's said something to her behind my back.

"I'm going to shoot off now," she says, looking like she wants to be anywhere other than here.

"What? No, don't go. It's early. Stay for breakfast."

"I don't know. I've left Norm all night. I've never, ever done that before. I feel terrible. I should have just gone straight home after the pub."

This explains her temperament. No wonder she's quiet. But it's not just that. It's not.

"Okay, well let's go then," I say, standing up and brushing my clothes down, "just give me a minute to have a quick wash, and I'll be with you."

"There's no need, George, honestly. I tell you what, why don't you just stay here and chill, and maybe we can meet up later for dinner."

Is this a brush off?

"It's okay. I won't be long, I promise."

Iris sighs. I know exactly what's coming.

"Please, George. It's fine. Stay here. I'll call you when I'm back."

"What's the matter with her?" Adam says under his breath as Iris hurries quickly out the door.

I bid farewell to her but receive no such reply. I glare at Adam. If looks could kill, he'd be dead right now.

"What did you do?" I growl at him.

"Me? Nothing," he smiles.

"Fuck you, Adam."

"Christ, what's boiling your piss this morning?"

I could smash that snide smile right off his face. He's always been good at this, playing games with me. I used to like that little smirk of his. It was pretty sexy. I knew it would lead to something… nice. Now, it's making me feel physically sick.

"I don't know what you've said, or done to her, but I swear to you I'll find out and you won't know what the fuck has hit you."

"Ooh, resorting to threats now, are we?"

72

Those eyes, they're staring into the deepest depths of my soul. They're saying, "Mom, where have you been? Fancy leaving me all on my own while you go out gallivanting with your fancy-man." And those eyes, they're right. And I don't think I've ever felt so guilty in all my life.

I kneel down and pull him into a cuddle, squeeze him tight. And with just that single gesture, all is right between us again. I can see he's forgiven me already.

I lock the door behind me, throw my keys in the bowl and head through to the kitchen. I unlock and fling open the back door and giggle as Norm waddles through it, in no rush for his morning constitutionals even though he's been left for a long time.

I slump onto my reading chair and replay the last hour or so in my head. Is Adam right? Am I just another notch on George's bedpost? It doesn't feel like that, not to me, and if I am, he's a bloody good actor.

No. It's not George that's the problem here. There was a palpable air of tension last night and Adam was right in the thick of it. He's the issue, no one else. Maybe he likes things just the way they are. Maybe he doesn't want anyone from the outside in. I don't know and to be honest, I don't care, but I still think it's best if I never go back to their place again.

73

Well, that's a relief. I'd got this funny feeling that I wouldn't be hearing from Iris again, let alone today. Her text was apologetic, and it seems I was worrying over nothing. I'm still not happy with Adam. I still believe he's had a hand in unnerving her, but her text said nothing about him. I think she was just really worried about leaving Norm.

I start having the wash I was going to have this morning. I've got a reason to now.

"Off out, are we?" Adam says, standing outside the bathroom door.

"Yup," I say, brushing past him on the landing.

He grabs my right arm by the wrist, pulls me backwards and pushes me against the wall. He's got a crazy look in his eyes. I used to like it.

"What is it, George? What is it about Iris?"

"Not that I need to answer that, but I'm really into her. That's all I have to say. Now, let me get ready will you?"

Adam shakes his head, laughing.

"She's a pathetic, misery of a woman, George. She's got no go in her. I've seen more personality in a tea bag."

A red mist washes over me and I feel like I'm burning up, ready to explode.

"You want to say that again, mate? Go on. I dare you!"

"Why? What're you going to do about it?"

He doesn't want to know. Seriously doesn't want to.

"Just get out of my face. I'm warning you."

Adam's face inches closer, makes me feel claustrophobic.

"Why would you want her when you've got me?"

"Adam, I love you. You're my best mate, you always will be but I don't want you."

"You used to."

"So, we had a few moments. That's all in the past. It's history, dude."

"Not for me. Don't deny this. You still feel it, don't you?"

I shake my head. No, I don't feel it, not anymore. At one time, I did think what we had was more than just friendship. Maybe I couldn't tell the difference. Maybe the signals were confused. Up until him, I'd never had a best friend. Never had friends, truth be told.

The look on Adam's face isn't anger, it's not love. His eyes aren't pleading with mine. He looks empty. Despondent. Like he doesn't care. I don't know how to compute it. I don't know what to do next. There's nothing I can say.

His arms drop to his sides, hang limply. He turns on his heel and silently walks away.

74

Well, that's a relief. I'd got this funny feeling that I wouldn't be hearing from George again, not after how I behaved earlier. I mean, I wasn't nasty, but I hurt him. I hope he knows how sorry I am. Can you gauge that kind of a thing over a text message?

I hope he comes around; hope he accepts the olive branch I've offered. I know I said we could go out for dinner, but I've promised Norm that I won't be going anywhere today. I hope George still wants dinner with me.

I start having a proper wash. It was just the bare basics this morning. I can take more time on my regime now.

I've got a joint of lamb in the slow cooker, bathing in garlic, rosemary and red wine. It smells divine and you know what, even if George decides to stay away, me and Norm have got one hell of a feast to look forward to.

George looks good. Possibly too good, especially seeing as we're not going out now.

He sniffs the air, sighs contentedly.

"Lamb, right?" he asks again.

"It is."

"Perfect," he says but he's not looking at dinner, he's looking at me.

75

The unmistakable smell of lamb and garlic and wine fills my head and it takes everything in me to stop myself salivating. Norm is the animal equivalent of me, right now, although I'm not sitting, staring up at the slow-cooker, ready and waiting.

I realise quickly that we're not going out for dinner. I look over at the dining table to find it set out for the occasion and I feel bad. If I would have known we were staying in for dinner, I would have bought a bottle of wine. Maybe two.

I'm not saying that Iris doesn't look amazing, she always does to me, but I feel ever so slightly overdressed. I would have preferred her to tell me we were eating in, just so I could dress to suit, but never mind, I'm here and I'm sure I'll forget about my attire soon.

"I'm sorry," I say, bringing her attention to my over-the-top clothing with a casual wave of my hand, "I thought we were going out, hence the outfit."

"Don't be silly, George. You look great. I'm sorry we're not going anywhere though, I really am. It's just that Norm was left alone for ages yesterday and…"

"Please, it's okay, honestly," I say, pull her into a hug, "this is amazing. Thank you."

Iris smiles at me. I smile back. And I can't think of anything more wonderful.

"That was delicious," I say between Norm's whimpered pleading for what little I've left on my plate.

"Thank you. I'm so glad you enjoyed because I feel like I've let you down."

"What? No," I say, shaking my head, "this is perfect."

Iris blushes, quickly takes a sip of her wine.

Norm's eyes feel like they're boring into the back of my skull. He pads the floor with his paws impatiently.

"Sorry, he's always like this whenever there's food around, even if it's just the tiniest scrap," Iris giggles, "just put your plate on the floor, and yes, before you say it, I'm a bad Mum."

"Hey, our old faithful, Sally, lived to the ripe old age of eighteen," I comfort her, "and she ate pretty much anything and everything that was going. Everything in moderation."

"Oh, you didn't tell me you had a dog. What breed?"

"Staffy," I say, looking at the smiling, tongue-out dog, waiting patiently, "just like Norm."

"Really? Wow. They're the best dogs, aren't they?"

I nod. She's right.

"I mean, I know they're bat-shit crazy and they have no idea what personal space is, and they stink to high heaven, but that's kind of what makes them so adorable. Well, not that last bit. The smells that come from her arse are so not adorable."

I nod, laugh.

"Did you get another dog after Sally passed away?"

"Well, I was about to move out when she died, so no."

"What about your parents?"

"No. My Mum was devastated," I say, my throat feeling thick with emotion, recalling the moment we had to have Sally put to sleep, "She vowed that was it. No more dogs. Said she couldn't go through the heartache again."

My eyes fill with tears, but I blink them away as I look up to Iris. She's crying.

"I'm sorry, Iris. I didn't mean to upset you."

"It's okay," she catches her breath, "It's not you. I'm just dreading it. Dreading the day I have to say goodbye to Norm. I don't think I'll cope."

"You will, I promise," I comfort her, "It just takes time, that's all. Losing your dog is like losing a human member of the family. In some way, it's almost worse. They love you unconditionally. They don't argue or talk back. They listen."

"I know," Iris cries hard, "He's my best friend, George."

I nod and make my way toward her. This woman needs one hell of a hug. I feel Iris sink into me, molding into the space between my arms.

"But he's not going anywhere," I breathe into her hair, "not yet. Not while he's got your fantastic cooking to enjoy."

Iris's shoulders shake in a half cry-half laugh. And now she's laughing.

"Thank you," she barely whispers.

Norm's turned his back on us. It's as if he's embarrassed. I look up and smile.

"What for?" I say.

"For being here. For saying the right thing," her face is tilting up, getting closer and closer to mine. I can't look anywhere other than at her pink, plump lips, "For…"

And she's kissing me.

And I'm kissing back.

76

I'm kissing him and he's kissing back, and I don't think I've ever felt so close to him, to anyone, ever. We wouldn't have talked if we went out, well not properly. This is exactly what we both need. Just each other. No one else.

If it was up to me, I'd stay like this forever, wrapped up in George, but I can feel him fidgeting, shifting his weight. He pulls away from me.

"Sorry, Iris, I need to piss."

I laugh. For a second there, I thought he was going to break some bad news.

"I'll let you off. Hurry up back though, won't you?" I say as suggestively as I can.

George rises and walks quickly to the toilet. I think he'd probably run, given the chance.

Something drops from his pocket, catches my eye. It's square and off-white in colour. I squint slightly, trying to focus better. It's a folded piece of paper. There's writing on it, well, it looks like there is.

I look up in the direction of the toilets, and very quickly, unfold it. I allow my eyes to skim over it. The handwriting is unmistakable. I'd know it anywhere.

77

The look on Iris's face screams anger. How, and why, her demeanor has changed so quickly, is beyond me. And then she holds up my letter. Oh fuck!

"What the hell is this, George?"

I tell her I can explain. Everything.

"You bastard!" she bellows.

"I'm sorry," is all I can muster.

"You're sorry? Is that all you have to stay to me?"

I tell her there's nothing more I can say. I tell her we need to talk.

"Oh, do we now?"

"Please, Iris."

"No!" she shouts between clenched teeth, "Go away. Go home. Goodnight, George."

In one swift, cutting moment, I realise that I have ruined everything.

78

This is why I'm better off alone, single. It takes so much for me to trust anyone, especially men. But George has wormed his way into my head, and heart. He was starting to be part of my life. Well, he's blown that all to hell.

I really thought we had something. I've never let myself get so close to someone so quickly, especially of the opposite sex. I've been burned before and didn't ever want it to happen again.

Everything felt so right with George though. Okay, we hadn't been together long but there was an instant, natural connection, a meeting of minds. It felt organic, different. It was good.

I should have known something was going to happen, but this? This is beyond anything I could ever have imagined. He must have known that, at some point along the road, he'd get found out.

I'm devastated. If there's one person I really could have had a relationship with, it was him.

And now he's ruined everything.

79

It was always going to happen. I should have stopped. What the hell was I thinking?

80

I used to hate Sunday evenings as a kid because it was always school the next day. I hated Mondays even more because the bullies had had a whole weekend away from me and were always ready, all guns blazing, to pepper me with yet another tirade of abuse.

I've got almost the same feeling now, a mixture of dread and fear. I'm not a kid anymore, but that isn't stopping me from feeling like one.

LUCY ONIONS

81

I couldn't bear Sundays as a kid. I used to get butterflies in my stomach, pangs of nervous nausea. I dreaded what the next day would inevitably bring. It's cliché, I know, but the mental abuse hurt way more than the physical.

I've got that same feeling again, the anxious wait. The fear and dread. But this time, it's no one's fault but mine. I know what I've put Iris through is irreparable and I'll never forgive myself for it.

82

I can't. I just can't face work today. I don't think I can deal with seeing his face. It'll kill me.

I just want to hide. Crawl under my duvet, and never come back out. I know, I'll build myself a pillow fort! I'll grab some books, some provisions – you know, the essentials, and I won't come out until the storm is over. Yes, my mind is made up. Time to phone work. I'll tell my boss I'm ill because I don't think telling her I'm heartbroken will go down to well.

My boss must have taken some happy pills or something because she was very understanding. I wasn't expecting such a favourable response.

George has phoned in sick too. She didn't seem that bothered about that either. The fact that two of her minions are "apparently" ill. I don't know what's got into her, and frankly, I don't care. I'm more concerned that George isn't at work. If he's thinking of coming calling, he's going to find himself in a world of fucking pain. If I so much as see his face, someone better stop me from clawing his eyes out.

My phone buzzes on silent, the screen lights up.

"Are you there?"

Oh, I'm here alright! Doesn't mean I'm going to answer you though, George.

Another message.

"Iris. Please?"

I pick my phone up. My head is screaming at me, don't even think about it! I unlock the device and shake my head as my fingers hover over the electronic, qwerty keyboard that appears as I tap the reply box. I must be stupid. I must be out of my head.

"I'm here," I type, and hesitate before I hit send.

"Oh, thank God. Thank you for replying. I know I'm the last person you want to speak to right now."

I laugh dramatically. You're not wrong, George!

"You are correct," I tap quickly.

"I'm so sorry, Iris. I don't know what's wrong with me."

Oh, I do, George. You're a psycho!

"What do you want me to say?"

"I know. I know."

"No. You. Don't!" I type immediately, then, "you haven't got a clue!"

"Can we talk?"

"We are!"

"No. I mean really talk. I need to speak to you. Properly."

"I don't want to see you. I don't want you anywhere near me."

"I'll call you. Can I do that?"

"Whatever!"

My heart feels like it's going to explode out of my chest. What the hell am I doing? You know what? I should have phoned the police as soon as I realised the letters were becoming a thing. When I started getting them. Any normal person would have done that. It's stalking. That's what it is. He's been in my house. Long before I allowed him entry. I should have done something, right then. But…

No, don't even think it, Iris!

But, I kind of liked them. The letters. That's how sad I am. I mean, they freaked me out. Of course they did, but they never felt overly threatening. I almost liked the attention, the mystery. They made me feel like a character in a book, or a movie.

What are you saying, Iris? You realise how desperate you sound, right?

My phone rings and I throw it to the floor in shock, so lost in my thoughts I'd forgotten he was going to phone me.

"Hey," I say, wondering if George can hear the sound of my heart racing.

"Hey," he replies, "Iris, I'm so, so sorry."

"Yeah. Change the record!"

83

I know, no matter how many times I tell her I'm sorry, she'll never forgive me, but that's all I say. I'm sorry. I'm sorry. I'm sorry. Sit at the back and write it out one hundred times.

I suggest we meet up, expect her to tell me to fuck right off, so imagine my surprise when she agrees. I get the feeling that we've both said enough. I can hear it in her voice, and I'm just done. Mentally and emotionally exhausted. If I'm feeling like this, I can't imagine what she's going through.

84

I'm looking at myself in the bathroom mirror, and I'm sure my reflection has just shaken her head at me.

What the hell, Iris! A date?

"It's not a date," I shout back at her, "and anyway, you have no idea!"

Oh, I do, and you, my dear, are being very silly.

"I just need to hear him out. When I want your advice, I'll ask for it."

I splash water on my face, hoping the cold water will wash away my thoughts. I look back at the mirror, and it's just me, looking back at me. I'm going crazy. I'm actually going crazy. But this crazy person needs to retreat to her pillow fort and lock the world out, if only for a little while.

I don't want him here; I've decided that much. I want to meet him. We do need to talk. I want to find out what the hell he thinks he's playing at.

I pick my phone up and start to text him. I tell him it's best we meet on neutral ground. Pub it is then.

85

I order Iris a beer, hoping she'll approve because, tonight, the cider isn't on. I scope out a booth, away from the bar, right at the back of the pub. I text her to let her know of my whereabouts within the heaving room.

I'm nervous. I'm not afraid to admit it. I glance at my watch, noting that half an hour has passed already, and I've finished my beer. I look at Iris's full pint glass, watch as drops of condensation weave their paths down the length of it. I could just pick it up right now, pick it up and down the cool contents, and then, from the corner of my eye, I see her standing there, her arms crossed over her chest.

"You're not going to drink that, are you?" she asks.

I smile widely, eagerly, and realise this will not be the happiest of meetings.

"Iris, you're here."

"Of course I am. It was my idea, wasn't it?"

I nod my head, tell her that I wouldn't have been surprised if she stood me up.

"It's not a date, George. I hope you don't think I'm here for the fun of it."

Ouch.

She pulls off her green parka jacket and sits down

opposite me. She picks up the pint glass, polishing off the beer in no more than a few mouthfuls.

"Man, I needed that!" she says, wiping her arm across her mouth.

Does she have any idea how damn sexy she looks?

"Want another?"

"Yup!"

"Thank you," she says sharply as I put our drinks on the table and take my seat. I look at her then straight back down at my drink.

"So, have you been off work all week, then?" she says, bluntly.

I nod.

"Couldn't face it?" she asks again.

"No."

"Strangely enough, neither could I."

I tell her I'm shocked. She's not one to have a lot of time off work, well not in one chunk, at least.

"I know, right? Being stalked by your boyfriend-slash-work colleague kind of does that to you."

I can't disagree. I tell her I'm sorry. Again.

"So why didn't you stop?"

"I didn't think you'd find out who wrote them."

"Well, that's just stupid."

"I know."

"I mean, didn't you even think…"

"No. No, I didn't, and I'll never forget it for the rest of my life."

"Things could have been so good between us, George," she says, her face dropping in disappointment.

"I know, Iris. It's all my fault. I don't know what else I can say, or do, to make this any better."

Her eyes are boring into mine, searching them. I feel a lump forming in my throat, but I can't cry. I must not. She already thinks I'm the lowest of the low. Crying in front of her would be the final nail in the coffin.

"Drink?" she asks, letting out a small burp, and if I'm not mistaken, is that a smile?

LUCY ONIONS

86

I'm not drunk but the alcohol is beginning to have the desired effect. But what in the hell am I doing? I came here to have it out with him. I came here to draw a long, thick line under the whole thing. Didn't I? That's the whole purpose of tonight, isn't it?

I don't know though. I feel for him. Well, part of me does. I mean, the letters were never malicious. They freaked me out, don't get me wrong, but the content itself never scared me. If anything, and I still can't quite believe I'm saying this, I felt flattered. The one that made its way into my house, my home, that's just not right, and he knows it.

I order another two pints and I promise myself I won't drink mine so quick this time. I hand George his drink, and as if we're in some corny, cliched romance, our hands brush. Seriously?

I feel my cheeks flush, so I turn my face away and quickly sit down. I want to be angry. I really do.

LUCY ONIONS

87

I'm not drunk. Well, not really, but the alcohol is working its magic, making me feel just slightly more at ease. Why is she still here? I don't know. I know I wouldn't be if our roles were reversed. I'm certainly not going to ask her out loud because whatever we've got going on now will be destroyed.

"So how have you been this week?" she slurs slightly.

I tell her I've been better.

"Ditto."

An awkward silence fills the air between us.

"So, what happens now?" she asks, breaking it.

"I don't know," I tell her.

"Well, you need to stop with the letters, don't you?"

"I do. I will. You know I will," I assure her and I'm starting to wonder what she's going to say next. I've got a feeling it's going to be more promising than I deserve.

"Right, get your coat."

88

That's it, I have definitely lost it. I should be running a mile, not trying to get closer to a man who thinks it's perfectly fine to terrorise a woman, but I think he is honestly, truly sorry, and I miss him. I miss us. In my head, it sounds utterly ridiculous. But you hardly know him, not really, it's saying. It wasn't exactly a relationship, was it?

My heart totally disagrees.

"Are you sure about this?" George asks me timidly.

I tell him it's fine, turning the key in the lock of my front door. It opens, and I walk in. This is like the worst case of déjà vu. Here we are again, only this time, George isn't budging an inch.

"Come on, then," I order, and he obeys.

Norm excitedly runs circles in front of me. I pat his head and give him a good scratch behind his ears. George reaches out to do the same, and although my trusty sidekick of a dog accepts the attention, I can see the little look in his eyes as he lets out a low rumble of a growl. That's my boy.

George takes his hand away quickly, sensing Norm's mood, and follows me into the kitchen.

"Beer? Wine?" I ask, placing my coat on the back of a chair.

"Wine, please."

I take out two glasses and grab a bottle of wine from the rack. Norm scampers in to us. I'm certain he thinks I only come in here to make him food. Seriously, it's relentless. He's my shadow. He's only got to hear a drawer being pulled open, or the slam of the fridge door and he's by my side in a shot.

I look down at him, and on cue, he sits his backside down, lifts his paw. And those eyes? He's got this act nailed. He knows I'll always give in. I grab a tin of dog food, open it. It stinks to high heaven. I empty the contents into his bowl. He cries and whimpers as if he's never been fed. It drives me insane; he drives me insane, but I know I'd be lost without him.

Ah, wine!

I pour, put our now full glasses on the table, and finally, we sit down. George is staring in awe at Norm.

"Blimey, that dog can eat!" he says.

We start laughing. Norm lets out a huge belch, and with a visibly full stomach, he trundles away and takes up residence in his favourite spot – the rug in front of the fire. It's not on, the fire, but still, he settles down.

We fall into another awkward silence, both taking long, deep gulps of our wine.

"So, are we friends again?" George asks hopefully.

Are we? I guess this means we are. I wouldn't have asked him back here if we weren't.

"I suppose it does," I say, "but seriously, no more letters. No more stalking around."

He nods eagerly, reminds me a little of Norm. Anything to please me.

"I mean it, George!"

"I know. I promise."

89

I insisted on calling a taxi. Insisted I would go home. She was having none of it though.

This sofa is pretty comfortable actually, considering the mountain of bed clothes she's given me. I'm surprised I even managed to get even close to lying down, but I did, and I slept like a baby.

I wasn't expecting this. I thought I'd gone and truly fucked it all up, and now I know I haven't, and I've got to do as she says. I mean, I've promised her. No more letters. I'm not so sure I can stick to my word. Not sure at all.

90

"Sleep well?" I ask George, who seems to be having a fight with the coffee pot.

"I did. Very well, thank you. You?"

Actually, no, I haven't slept well at all. I would have done if he'd been lying there next to me. I'm not about to tell him this though. I just nod.

"You look tired," he says, handing me a mug of steaming hot coffee, "Here, drink."

I'm not going to argue. I am, so very tired, and even though I would have been offended had anyone else told me I "looked tired", I know that George is sincere. I can tell he is.

I take a sip from my mug and sigh contentedly.

"Iris, I've got to shoot off soon, okay?" he says, glum.

"No worries," I lie, secretly hoping he'll stay, "What you up to?"

Way to go, Iris. Sure fire way of turning a guy off.

"Well, it's safe to say I'm not going anywhere near work, and I'm expecting a delivery."

I nod, and mentally urge myself to keep my mouth shut. I'm not his Mother. He doesn't need to tell me anything.

91

I wave to Iris as I step out onto the pavement. I know it's going to take her a while to trust me again but last night, well, it's a good start.

Of course, there's no delivery. I made that up. I could have stayed with her, but I want to be back home. I need to write. I need to preserve the way I'm feeling on paper.

I've always kept a diary, but since I've been writing the letters, and, for the want of a better word, stalking Iris, I've neglected it. That ends today. I've got so much to tell it. So much has happened since I last made an entry. It needs my full attention, a few hours, and a bottle of wine.

2

1

"Is that the last of it?" I shout to George. His face has turned a deep red, droplets of sweat forming on his brow. His legs are shaking, threatening to buckle under the weight of the huge, overfilled box he's grasping on to.

"Yup," he manages to squeeze the word through gritted teeth and drops the box right inside the doorway. He doubles over, hands clutching his knees, sucks in as much air as he can.

If you would have asked me, all those ten and a half months ago, if I'd ever have George living with me, I would have laughed in your face, and told you to kindly get lost. Yet here he is. Under my roof, or should I say, *our* roof. With him paying half to everything, it'll free up some funds for me, and more than anything else, he'll be company.

I lost Norm three months ago. A mixture of old age and a brain tumour, detected just a few weeks before he passed away. I'm not scared to admit, I struggled. Still do. He was my best friend. Some people would think that pathetic – how can you count an animal as your best friend? The answer is, you can. You do. Anyone who has, or has had a dog, will tell you exactly the same. I miss the sound of the tip-tapping of his claws on the kitchen floor. I miss the heat and comfort of having him sleep at the end of the bed, his head keeping my feet toasty. I miss his legs going ten-to-the-dozen, lost in dreams. I miss his smile. Yes, that's right. Dogs smile. Norm did the majority of the time. I miss our chats. I miss him.

I needed to fill the emptiness with something, someone. Of course, that's not the only reason I asked George to move in. It's not all about the financial benefit, or companionship, although they both help a great deal. It's about love. I love him.

George appears at the bottom of the stairs looking happily exhausted.

"All done," he says as he slumps down onto the sofa he used to sleep on.

I haven't told him about my trip to the supermarket. Haven't mentioned the bottle of champagne, and a box of luxury chocolates, so as I pop the cork and pour out two flutes of the fizzy stuff, his eyes light up.

"You didn't have to," he says, takes a sip and raises his glass.

"I know," I say, and we toast to our future.

2

I'm still pinching myself to be honest. I mean, I'm so glad to be here, but I can't quite believe what's happening. It's taken Iris so much to let me back into her life, to trust me again. I seriously thought I'd blown it. I didn't hold out any hope of getting back together, let alone move in with her. I'm shocked, surprised but so fucking happy.

She's bought champagne. Shit! Why didn't I think of that? I don't often, well, ever, drink the stuff for the following reasons: It's expensive, and I've not had all that much to celebrate in my life. Up until now.

I close my eyes and feel the bubbles slide down my throat, and then I open them to see she's finished hers already. She's smiling. Not just any old smile. This one is weighted with cheeky, playful promise, and it can only mean one thing.

3

I feel different. Last night was intense. It wasn't just sex, it was so much more. It's eight am, and I don't know why I'm awake so early, especially as it's a Saturday, but I am, and I feel refreshed. Renewed. Revived.

I left George sleeping. I'm surprised I managed to drag myself away. It was so hard to stop staring at that beautiful face of his, but my stomach was making itself known with deep, loud gurgles, and that's why I'm here, in the kitchen, sorting out something for breakfast.

I'm so glad we arranged for George to move in yesterday rather than today. At least now we've got a couple of days before we hit reality. I say *reality* because none of this has sunk in yet. It just feels like he's staying over, like we're playing house. I'm sure that'll change soon enough.

"Morning," George croaks, looking more gorgeous than ever.

LUCY ONIONS

4

I feel... different. In a good way. A really good way. Last night was incredible. It wasn't just sex. It was so much more.

I can't help but stare at her pottering around. I've sat here, watching her do this before, but it feels *official* now. This is my home now too.

Iris dishes up steaming, scrambled eggs on to hot, buttered toast. She puts our plates on the table, sits down across from me, and smiles. She tells me to tuck in, so I start. I can feel her eyes on me. She doesn't seem to be touching her food, and for a second, I feel awful. I look up at her, and she shakes her head, as if pulling herself out of a daydream. She smiles again, and starts to eat.

I clear my plate. The eggs were delicious, and if I didn't feel so full, I'd definitely eat some more.

I'm glad all the unpacking, and upheaval, was dealt with yesterday. Yes, it was a long bloody day, and yes, we were both done-in (I'm amazed that we did anything but sleep once we actually got to bed), but it's all done.

5

It would have been so much easier to stay in, in our pj's, doing absolutely nothing, all day, but I'm glad we've made the effort.

We haven't got the stuff in for dinner, so going to the pub for lunch seems a no brainer. It's the weekend and I plan on making the most of it before we go back to work.

George is cleaning all the breakfast things away, and I almost stop him, after all, I'm used to it. But I stand back and let him get on with it. It's *our* home now.

I wash and get changed into an outfit that's smart but casual. It's a pub lunch, not haute cuisine. I put on just enough makeup to hide the bags under my eyes and give myself the once-over in the mirror. Not too bad really, considering I hardly slept last night.

I hear footsteps on the stairs, heading towards the room. A jolt of excitement hits me, pulses through me, and I feel my heart rate increase.

Chill out, Iris. Relax.

The door opens and George appears, his eyes fixed on me. The look on his face suggests he's thinking of one thing, and one thing only. I feel my cheeks burn with the thought.

He says nothing as he walks past me, towards the

wardrobe. He is silent as he pulls his clothes from hangers. I know something is going to happen. I can feel it.

He drapes his clothes over my vanity table chair, turns and looks at me. His eyes don't stray an inch as he pulls his pyjama top over his head, don't falter as he pulls his shorts down. I gulp. I wonder if he can hear my blood pumping as loud as I can.

He slides up to me, asks me why I'm already changed. I tell him it's because we're going out for dinner. And then, if he couldn't be any hotter, he tells me he fancies a little appetiser first.

6

Christ, she looks good! I know she's made an effort, but, and I mean this in the best possible way, it doesn't look like it. Considering all the hard labour we put in this weekend, she looks fresh, and natural, and downright bloody gorgeous. I know she's all changed and ready to go, but I just can't help myself.

I push her onto the bed. Her breath catches, and her cheeks flush red. I kneel over her, allowing my eyes to take in every inch of her. She may be fully clothed, but I know exactly what lies beneath the slim, slip of fabric that ends just above her knees.

I gently roll her dress up, just a fraction. Her breath catches again. I roll it up a little more, adjust my position, and a little bit more again until I reach her thighs. I kiss them both, just on the inside. She wriggles and writhes beneath me.

She wants the dress off, of that I am sure. She tugs at it, tries to pull it over head. I stop her. Not yet, I tell her, and she nods.

I roll the dress up to her chest and trail kisses up her stomach. I look up to see her eyes roll, her lids flickering, and I know I've got her.

7

We're still holding hands as we approach the pub. I'm not one for public displays of affection as a rule, then again, before George, there was no one really to be affectionate with. Neither of us has said much at all, and yes, I know this sounds cliché, but it feels like the first moment we met. I don't know why, but my stomach is doing somersaults. I know he's been looking at me, I keep catching him in the act.

The pub isn't heaving, but it's pretty busy, bustling with chat and clinking glasses. I love the atmosphere here.

I spot a cosy little nook at the back of the room, and almost pull George along, hoping no one else is about to claim it. We're surrounded by people, but sitting here, in this little cocoon, consisting of a table and sofa, I feel like we're all alone.

I'm ravenous, and could happily manage two dinners to myself, but I just sit and stare at George, watch him looking at the menu intently. Does he know how good he looks? Does he know how much I love him?

I snap out of my trance as he asks me what I fancy. As in food, or…?

I go for fish and chips. He chooses something different,

bangers and mash, so "we can share".

He heads over to the bar to order. I love the way he walks. The way he shoves his hands in his pockets. He becomes very animated as he stands, waiting to order. It's clear he knows most of the people around him, behind the bar and before it.

I sit, and watch in wonder, as he chats away. He's not even ordered anything yet, too busy laughing at whatever the guy standing next to him has just said. And now the barman's involved. I wish I knew what they're on about. I'm not in the right position to lip read, or should I say, they're not, and the steady hum of numerous other conversations masks any other sound.

He's finally ordering, or at least, I think that's what he's doing. He turns around, drinks in hand, his face beaming.

He excuses himself from his small, but captivated audience. And that's what he is. Captivating. He's wearing his hair down today. I don't particularly mind the buns, but thankfully, I think he's got the message that I love those long, thick, brown curly locks, down, just brushing his shoulders. He tucks his hair behind his left ear, and even that simple, natural movement, has me thinking about things that make my face flush. I smile and do my best to compose myself as he sits back down.

He asks me if I'm okay. I tell him I'm fine, not that I'm feeling a little hot and bothered. I excuse myself and head to the ladies.

8

I'm interrupted from ogling Iris, forced to take my eyes off her body as she walks towards the toilets, by Adam and Lucas.

"How did the move go?" Lucas asks me.

"Well, I'm in."

"Yeah, and don't we know it!" Adam snipes.

I ask him what that's supposed to mean, ask him what the problem is.

"Shut up, Adam!" Lucas tells him.

"Don't tell me to shut up, you prick!"

"I don't know what the hell is going on, but whatever it is, I don't like it!"

"Guy's, come on," I step in.

My two friends slip into silence.

It's awkward.

Very awkward.

"But you're all moved in and sorted?" Lucas asks, clearly trying to ease the tension.

"Yeah. It's exhausting though, that's for sure. This weekend has felt like a mini lifetime."

"Any arguments yet?" he asks again, looking across at Adam, who seems to be biting his tongue.

I laugh, tell him no, not yet.
He smiles, no, smirks, and I'm not sure I like it.

9

It feels like I haven't seen Adam and Lucas in an age, and that's ridiculous. We still work in the same department. That being said, I did everything I could to avoid them when I split up with George. And they kept their distance too, as much as it was possible to. It's good to see them though. Good to see the three of them sitting together.

"Hi, guys," I say, taking my seat.

"Hi, Iris," Adam and Lucas say in unison.

I look at George. There's something… off. He really doesn't look like he wants to be here.

"Been in long?" Adam asks.

"Not really. We thought we'd come for dinner. There's no way I'm setting foot near an oven today. We haven't stopped have we, George?"

Adam sniggers.

Lucas looks like he could kill him.

George looks well and truly pissed off.

"Is something the matter?" I ask all three of them.

"I don't know. Is there, Adam?" George says.

"Fucking hell, Adam! What's your problem?" Lucas shouts.

"I haven't got one."

"Really?" Lucas says.

"Really," Adam shoots back.

"You could have fooled me. Anyway, I think it's best we leave," Lucas says, getting up to go, pulling at Adam's shirt sleeve.

"Enjoy your dinner," Adam spits, and follows Lucas out the pub.

I look at George, shake my head, the voice inside it asking, "what the fuck?"

10

There's a distinct air of tension between us, and for what reason, neither of us know. Well, we do kind of know. Adam's attitude. What the hell is his problem?

Our meals are put in front of us, the smell of them causing my mouth to water. I look at Iris, and she seems as eager as me to tuck in.

"Oh my God. You would not believe how much I need this!" she says.

Yes. The atmosphere has been cut, for the better, and all because of food.

She's poised over her plate, knife and fork at the ready. She's waiting for me to make the first move, so I start to eat and that's all it takes.

"That was amazing," Iris says, dropping her cutlery and letting out a long breath.

"It was," I agree, "think you can squeeze in a desert?"

"Oh, I don't know. I think I'll explode if I eat any more."

"Go on," I urge her, making a last-ditch attempt.

"Okay then, if I must," she giggles, "You're a bad influence, George!"

.

11

I really, really don't need to eat any more, but the temptation is just too much. I always crave something sweet and naughty after a big dinner, no matter how full I feel.

Whatever tension that was between us earlier, although why there was any in the first place is beyond me, has disappeared. I'm glad about that.

Our plates get taken away, and George goes back up to the bar to order dessert, and that leaves me to think, albeit briefly. I'm going to confront Adam at work on Monday. I want to know exactly what he thinks he's up to. You can't go around behaving like that without an explanation.

LUCY ONIONS

12

I practically have to force the last morsel of dessert into my mouth. I cram it in with my spoon and hope to God it doesn't come back out. I feel sweat prick my forehead and pray Iris doesn't notice.

I look at her and manage a smile. She's sitting right back against her chair, holding her stomach.

"Wow," she says, letting out a laboured sigh.

"I know," I agree.

"I knew I'd struggle with it. I shouldn't have even tried."

Iris's plate is clear, apart from a few crumbs and a little melted ice cream.

"You did though. You ate it," I laugh.

"Erm, so did you!"

I can't deny it.

"Was it worth it?" she asks, breaking into giggles.

"That's really not the point," I laugh again, "So, I assume another beer is out of the question?"

Her face turns pale, and ever so slightly green. She shakes her head, eyes closed.

"Can we just go home?" she says, and I really can't think of anything I want more.

13

My clothes feel like I'm going to have to literally peel them off. I feel fat and bloated, like a beached whale. I want to keep the lights off, wear my oversized nightie. I want to get into bed and sleep.

I turn the cold tap on and rinse my toothbrush. I look at my face in the mirror and seriously wonder why anyone would ever want... this.

I have these moments often, these times when I feel totally worthless. When I feel that no one in their right mind would ever want me. It's not that I think I'm disgusting or anything, and I'm not overweight, but that doesn't stop the insecurities getting the better of me.

I press the button on the electric toothbrush and close my eyes as it buzzes to life. I don't know why I do it. I just do.

The last thing I want is a night of romance, but I don't stop George from trailing his hands down my back. I don't bat them away as he grabs my waist and turns me around. I don't even put up any kind of resistance as they lift me up, and pull my legs around his waist, and I certainly don't put up a fight to stop them from what they're about to do.

14

And just like that, it's the last day of the weekend. I did suggest we go to the pub, again, this time for Sunday dinner. I thought it would be a good idea, seeing as we've only the bare basics in. But then I saw Iris's face drop, so we've decided on a not-going-out day. Probably for the best, what with work tomorrow.

We have books, music and wine, and we'll dine on Chinese take-away.

LUCY ONIONS

15

We wish the week away, will it to hurry up and then when Sunday comes, we wonder why we feel so deflated.

Where I'm usually a sucker for a Sunday dinner, when George suggested we go to the pub for it, I felt my heart drop. No. Not again. Not today.

It would be the easiest thing to do. We have literally enough for breakfast tomorrow. Nothing fancy, just cereal, bread, butter and juice. That's it.

What we do have plenty of is wine, books and records, and I'm sure if I flutter my eyes enough, we might even get a take-away.

16

W hy can't the weekend last longer? My alarm wakes me at the same time it does every weekday morning, but right now it feels like I've not slept a wink since it last went off. My own fault, I know. We were both exhausted last night. What we should have done was gone straight to bed. Well, we did. Not to sleep though. I couldn't help it, couldn't resist.

Iris moans and writhes in the throws of waking up.

"What?" she slurs, "No. Please tell me this is a bad dream? Tell me it's not Monday?"

"It's Monday," I confirm sadly.

She throws a pillow at my head, mutters words that are indescribable to me. I smile.

"You think it's funny, do you?" she says and kicks her legs off the side of the bed.

I shake my head, barely keeping laughter at bay.

"Well, I don't," she continues childishly.

"Neither do I! I mean, who likes Monday's anyway?"

"Shut up, George. Stop being so bloody cheerful."

I tell her I'm not. I'm lying.

"You are! I'd be cheerful if I'd had a proper night's sleep."

"I'm sorry," I giggle, "It was a nice way to lose a couple of hours though, wasn't it?"

"A couple of hours?" she laughs loudly, "Erm, okay. Whatever you say."

"Excuse me, what are you implying?"

"Just shut up. Let's get some breakfast and get ready."

17

I tell George to go in ahead of me. I don't know why. It's not as if our work mates don't know he's moved in with me. It's not a secret, although, at the same time, it's got nothing to do with anyone else anyway. I just know the reception we'll get if we walk in those doors together.

There's a couple of manuscripts on my desk. That's it. I kind of wish there were more. At least then I can use the fact that my head is stuck in one of them as an excuse to not talk to people.

I drop my bag to the floor beside me, boot my computer up, and look over to see George going through the same routine. He catches my eye and beams at me. I smile back.

He breaks his gaze, looks from me to his monitor.

And then his face changes.

He doesn't look so happy now.

18

This is a joke, right? It has to be, but it looks way too real. My screensaver has been changed. Someone has been tampering. Unless I've left it on all weekend, and... No, I wouldn't have. I've never done it.

It's not graphic, nothing rude or horrific, the image on the screen, but it's pretty bloody weird. It's of me and Iris in the pub on Saturday, sitting there, enjoying our food. It's been taken from the right-hand side of her. Surely, I would have noticed. Wouldn't I have seen, known, if someone was snapping away at her? Maybe they used a telephoto lens or something. That's even worse. I shudder.

I'm trying to think if I've ever given my password out. My mind draws a blank. No. It's not something I'd do anyway.

Actually, the management have a full list of our passwords. I guess they keep that kind of information in case they need to access our computers. But how would the boss have got this photo? And why? No. There's no way. It would be more than her job's worth.

Someone else has done this.

Someone in this office.

19

He's been quiet all morning, and that's not particularly concerning, but coupled with that shocked expression, well, something's off. Something's wrong.

It's lunchtime, and I need to find out what's going on. I head over to his desk and pull up a chair.

"Everything okay?" I ask.

"Yeah. Cool."

His tone and body language tell me something very different.

"George?"

"Iris?"

"Come on. I know something's up."

"Seriously, I'm fine," he snaps.

I get up to leave.

"Are you coming out for lunch?" I ask.

"I'll stay here if that's okay. You don't mind, do you? I've got loads to do."

"Fine," I say, taking his answer way too much to heart. We may live together, we may be a couple, but he's entitled to his own space, to do what he wants, within reason.

"Do you want me to get you something?"

"No. I'm fine. Just sort yourself out. Thanks for asking

though."

He leans over, kisses my cheek. I stand up and head to the door, and as I open it, I look back at my boyfriend and really wish I could read minds.

20

I don't want to shut her out, but it's what I do. My defence mechanism when I'm anxious or worried. I keep it all in. Bottle it all up. I don't need to worry her, and this shit definitely would. It would freak her the fuck out, just like it's freaking me out.

I'm no angel, I know that, and maybe this is all karma. I'm having a taste of my own medicine. It hasn't really been all that long since I was making Iris's life hell, but one thing I never did was take photos. Not once. I didn't need to. I wanted to keep it old school. I liked having a pen pal, albeit one that could, or would never, reply. I waited and watched from the shadows, and yes, I know what I did was wrong. I enjoyed it immensely, but once I had her, now that I've got her, that's it. No more Mr. Stalker.

Part of me wants to tell her about this photo, part of me is too scared to ger her involved. She's in the photo, but I don't think she's the subject. I'm the subject.

I need to sort this myself. I'm not dragging her into anything like this ever again.

21

We log off and pack up at almost the exact same time. I've never wanted to get home so badly. I want to lock the front door behind us, shut the world out.

Apart from lunchtime, we haven't spoken a word to one another all day. Okay, we've had work to do, quite a bit, but our lack of communication has absolutely nothing to do with that.

We start to walk through town, still in silence. The atmosphere between us is all off, it could be cut with a knife. Just when I think there'll be no interaction between us at all tonight, he takes my hand, holds it tight. It's warm, comforting. I look down at our interlocking fingers and breathe a silent sigh of relief. It's something, this small, simple gesture. It tells me we're okay.

George looks at me and smiles. It's contagious.

"I love you, Iris," he says.

"I know," I tell him.

22

Our self-imposed silence has been broken. Thank God. I know I wouldn't have been able to go all day without speaking to her, without touching her. All it took was for me to hold her hand.

I've never wanted to get home so much. I shut the door behind us, and at the same time, we sigh. It's one sound, not two.

Iris kicks her shoes off, leaves them were they lie. I know she'll pick them up and put them away before too long, but for now, she heads to the kitchen, and opens the fridge.

"Beer?" she calls through as I slump on to the sofa, not even bothering to take my jacket off.

"Please," I call back.

I hear the pop and fizz of bottles being opened, and I'm already imagining the taste and feel, the cold wetness, the first, well deserved mouthful.

Iris heads towards me and spots her shoes, and just as expected, she tuts and uses her right foot to push them up against the skirting board. Of course, this is only a temporary measure. They'll be put away properly soon.

She hands me a bottle and I throw my left arm over the top of the sofa, an unspoken invite to snuggle up next to me.

The only sound to be heard is that of swallowing beer. We both sigh again, and she wriggles down, filling the space at my side. Her eyes close and I feel a smile spread across my face. Nothing could be more perfect. I say a silent thank you, to who, I don't know, but I am thankful. For her. For us. For this.

"Are you sure everything's okay?" she says softly.

"I'm fine, I promise," I tell her, and I am. I'm more than fine.

"Good," she says as she leans up and kisses me.

She pulls away but doesn't take her eyes from mine. I can't look away, don't want to. She's got me.

She puts her bottle on the coffee table, then takes mine and does the same. The air between us is weighted with anticipation. This should be getting easier by now, shouldn't it? Should I still feel like it's the first time, every time? I fucking hope so.

She inches ever closer to my face and kisses me again, tentatively. She isn't pulling away this time, in fact, she's pressing into me so much, I'm surprised she's not gone through me.

Her hands are in my hair, and on my face. They're down on my chest, and now she's sitting on my lap. She breaks the bond our lips have made, and using both hands, pulls her top up over her head. I imagine most other guys would allow their eyes to travel downwards at this point, but I'm fixated by her eyes, like magnets. She leans in again, her mouth on mine, and she's fidgeting with something.

She swings her bra around her head like she's riding rodeo and giggles as she throws it across the room.

Iris collects her clothes from where they landed, gathering them into her arms. She stands, naked as the day she was born, and grins.

"I'm going for a shower. Feel free to join me for round two, if you think you can handle it," she says.

I throw my boxers at her and she runs up the stairs laughing. I pick my clothes up, might as well put them away when I get to our room, and I feel my phone buzz in the back pocket of my jeans.

There's a message notification on the screen. I swipe across to open it. I drop the phone and very nearly follow it to the floor.

This time, I know that whoever took this photo, has used some kind of zoom lens. It's not all that sharp, but it's sharp enough to make out what we were up to just moments ago. I know where it's been taken from. I know because I've been in this garden, I've hid behind that bush, just at the end of the stepping stone path.

I hear Iris scream. The sound feels like it's pierced my ear drums. I take the stairs two at a time.

She's slumped up against the wall, in the corner of the bathroom, next to the shower. She's still naked, dripping wet. She's sobbing, absolutely breaking her heart. Her eyes are wide, manic.

The shower is still running, and the steam it's producing is only just thin enough for me to see this terrible state my Iris is in.

I drop to the floor next to her. I ask her what the matter is, but she can't speak for crying. Instead, she points to the shower curtain.

I yank the glossy, wet plastic across. I don't notice anything obvious until I look down to the plug hole. There's a dog collar coiled, soaking up water, and it doesn't take a genius to realise who it belonged to.

23

hy?" I scream at him, "Why would anyone do this? How has someone done this?"

He shakes his head, keeps shaking it. I feel another wave of tears coming and I do nothing to hold them back. I must look such a mess, and I don't care. That's Norm's collar. That means someone has taken it. Someone has been in my loft, found my keepsake box, and took it. And then put it in the base of the shower. It's obviously not George. I've been in the same office as him all day. And anyway, he doesn't even know where my keepsake box is. No one does.

But then, maybe he does. Maybe he's been snooping. It's not like he doesn't know where the loft is. This is his house now too. He's got previous, hasn't he? And who, in their right mind, would strike up a relationship with their ex-stalker? A crazy person, that's who! Could he really be so callous, so evil, so nasty?

24

The slap to my face stings like hell.

"What the fuck?" I shout, rubbing my left cheek.

"Get out!" she screams at me.

"You don't think I…"

"Who else could it have been, George?"

I plead with her, tell her over and over that this was not me, tell her I would never, ever do anything like this. I know what a huge part of her life Norm was.

She begins to calm down, but looks so drained, so exhausted, so very fragile.

I take her into my arms, and she sinks into me.

"Well, who is it then?" she cries into my chest.

25

I've never felt so shaken by anything. Thankfully, George knows how to calm the storm. I shouldn't doubt him. Not anymore.

We're on our third beer each, and the way I'm feeling, I could keep going, carry on drinking the shock, and fear, and sadness away. It would be the easiest thing in the world to do right now, but in the back of my mind, a four-letter word lurks.

Work.

I don't want to feel like shit in the morning.

"Want another?" George asks.

I eagerly accept, all thoughts of work disappearing.

I slur as I tell George I'm going to bed and wish I would have eaten something a little more substantial than a packet of crisps.

"Me too," he says, tidying the last, four empty bottles away.

I wash, change and sink into bed. George follows suit. He sidles up behind me and I fit into him perfectly. I feel his left arm slide under my neck, his right arm around my waist.

I'm trying to close my eyes, but I can't. Someone has been

in my house. They haven't broken locks or windows. No sign of forced entry. How do I know they've gone? Could the perpetrator still be here, hiding away in the loft? We checked every room, but we didn't check that one.

George is lightly snoring, and I look at him, stare at him for a few moments. I need to make sure he's out for the count.

I slip out of his heavy grasp and tread lightly out of the room. My heart is pounding, feels like it's going to explode.

Why are you doing this, Iris? I ask myself. I feel sick with nerves but the only way I'll get any rest is by making sure there's no one, apart from us, in the house.

And what are you going to do if there's someone stowing away? Good question.

I creep downstairs and switch the lamp on that sits on the telephone table at the bottom. That's all the light I need. Any lighter, and it might wake George up.

Why didn't you wake George, Iris? I ask myself again. Safety in numbers and all that. What if something happens to me up there? What if something happens to George?

I take a deep breath, push my thoughts to one side, and pull a knife out of the block. I've never so much as punched anyone in my entire life. Not that I haven't wanted to on occasion. Would I really be able to use this if the shit hits the fan? Would I be able to stab someone?

Another deep breath.

I head back upstairs, tiptoe past my bedroom, to the far end of the landing. I place the knife on the bannister, take the long-handled hook from the spare room, and pull the loft hatch down, and then the three-tiered step ladder. I wince at the noise it makes, stand stock still for a second or two as I hear George mumble something in his sleep.

I pick the knife back up and gingerly ascend the steps. I can feel the ladder shaking in time with my body. I start to cry quietly, fear inching its way around me. I freeze momentarily.

Suck it up, Iris. You can do this.

With another, deep breath, I flick the light on, and the loft is bathed in a bright, warm glow.

There's nothing obvious. Nothing out of the ordinary. There's certainly no sign of anyone, or anything, setting up home here. Everything looks the same as when I last came up here.

Relief washes over me, and my body relaxes instantly. But there's still one last thing to check.

The lid of my keepsake box is on the floor next to it. Inside the box, on top of all my old photos and other memorabilia, is a folded piece of paper. My hands shake as I unfold it, and the words scribbled on it blur for a moment before they focus.

George,
Why are you doing this to me? Don't you know how much I love you? She doesn't. Not like I do. She never will. Leave now, before it's too late. Leave now so that we can be together forever.
Yours, always. xxxx

26

I can feel myself being pushed and pulled, backwards and forwards.

"What?" I shout, dazed and confused, wondering if I'm dreaming or wide awake.

"Wake up, George! Wake up!"

Iris is as white as a ghost, her eyes wide. My gaze drops to what she's got in her left hand, and now she realises I'm wide awake (how could I not be), she waves the paper in front of my face.

"It's for you," she says.

I snatch the letter from her hand.

I read. Every word. And then I read them again.

"What the fuck, George?" she shouts.

I'm speechless.

The hairs on my arms and neck stand on end.

Shit.

Fuck.

I can't even guess as to who the handwriting belongs to. Not a clue.

"Where did you find this?" I ask and know the answer before she replies.

"In my keepsake box. In the loft."

Iris starts to cry. I've never known her cry like this, cry so much. It's a horrible sound. On one hand, my heart is breaking for her. On the other hand, I really wish she'd calm down, stop. I pull her to me, hoping to quiet her.

"We'll phone the police," I tell her, "we've got to."

She nods.

I can feel her body going limp. She's exhausted. She slumps in my arms, and her breathing slows, barely audible. I won't sleep though. I don't think I've ever felt so angry.

27

I can't do this. Not again. Haven't I been through enough already? It's not fair.

I'm not going to tell George about the second letter. The one that wasn't addressed to him. The one in my dressing gown pocket. My fucking dressing gown pocket.

Iris,

How're you? Enjoying your live-in-lover catering to your every whim, I imagine. It should be me; you know. Me who's on the receiving end of all his affection. I mean, do you love him? Be honest.

Are you doing this on purpose? You are, aren't you. You don't want me to have him, but you don't necessarily want him either, especially after everything he's put you through.

You know what you are, don't you? Greedy. Jealous. It's not attractive, Iris. It's repulsive. You're repulsive.

It won't last.

Trust me.

I've had it. I can't take this shit anymore. This house doesn't feel like home, not now. It feels ruined, tarnished. It doesn't matter how many wonderful times I've had here; I can't stay. I'll take them with me wherever I go, wherever we end up next, but this place is dead to me now. And as much as that makes me so very sad, it's time to cut ties, to move on and make new memories.

28

She can't do this. Not again. Hasn't she been through enough already?

"It's not my home anymore, George. It's just a house," she cries quietly.

"It's all ruined, tarnished," she goes on, "and it doesn't matter how many wonderful times I've had here, I just can't stay."

I nod my head slowly, sympathetically, and pull her into my arms. I tell her that her memories won't leave her, that they're transferable, that this is all just bricks and mortar.

I feel moisture seep through my top onto my chest.

It's time to move on and make new memories. Together.

29

The only thing that stops me from throwing my phone across the room is the intense exhaustion I feel. I squint, repeatedly tap the snooze button, but I'm obviously missing it because that infernal alarm is still going. It's pointless snoozing now anyway. I'm awake. Christ knows how I've managed to sleep after last night, but I've had almost seven hours. I feel like shit, groggy and drained, and the thought of phoning in sick is growing more tempting by the second.

The smell of freshly brewed coffee hits me as I drag myself downstairs. I close my eyes, inhale deeply.

George is cooking our breakfast. We don't usually cook anything on a work day. We'd have to rush it, if we did. Cooked breakfasts are for lazy weekends.

"Hey," he says, holding a whisk aloft.

I walk up to him, lazily put my head on his chest.

"Looks great," I say, "but we'll have to hurry up or we'll be late."

"We don't have to hurry. We don't have to do anything at all," he says, turning his back to me, concentrating on not burning our food, "I've phoned work. I explained why we won't be in today. Told them we've got to wait in for a locksmith, who, incidentally, hasn't given us a set time slot."

He switches the gas off.

"Here you go," he says, putting my plate on the table.

I pull him to me and kiss him. What a legend.

I'm so grateful for the day off. My head, and my heart, wouldn't have been in it. I know it's only reading, but I don't think I'd be able to concentrate.

"Fancy getting out?" George says, "the fresh air will do us both good."

I smile, nodding in silent agreement.

I wash and change and put a little makeup on.

It still blows me away that you haven't got to go all that far to feel like you're in another world. Four miles away from home, and we're encompassed in a rural wonderland. It's idyllic and better than any medicine a doctor could prescribe. This, this is where I need to be. It's always been my dream to live in one of these cottages, in walking distance to a village, and a couple of cosy little pubs. Where everybody knows each other yet don't try to interfere too much. Where you're surrounded by rolling hills and moors, and the views, whatever the season, are nothing short of spectacular.

I want it more than anything, as long as George is by my side to enjoy it with me. I want to set up my own publishing house, rather than work for one. I want to spend more time on my own stories rather than those of other writers.

It will be a reality. I will make it so. And after what happened last night, and the times before, I'm more determined than ever. It's why I save, why I squirrel those last bits of money away once rent, bills and shopping have been paid for. Nothing will stop me making my dream come true.

Right on cue, we happen upon one of the three, village pubs, and seeing as it's almost lunchtime, it would be rude not to go in.

30

I t's not freezing outside, but cold enough that the log fire in the bar has been stoked up, its embers crackling in the hearth.

This is what it's all about for me. This is where I want, no, need, to be. The fact that all this rural beauty isn't too far out of town is pretty amazing. We could still commute, thanks to the bus, but hell, if the weather is on your side, you'd just walk. Why wouldn't you? You haven't got to go far to feel like you're in another world.

Iris is sitting in one of the chesterfield style armchairs by the fire, and the warm glow that's falling on her face makes her look even more beautiful. She looks happy, relaxed and I don't ever want that to change. I order a bottle of Malbec and join her.

As if we've just read each other's minds, we tell one another how much we want all this to be ours, this way of life. Her face beams as she sips her wine, and she tells me how she's been saving her money, how she would love nothing more than to share her dream with me, for us to live the rest of our lives in this little village.

She tells me her ultimate goal is to set up her own,

independent publishing house and concentrate on her own books, on getting them published.

She's animated, excited, and it's contagious.

We say nothing of the break in, knowing all it will do is ruin such a lovely afternoon.

We finish the bottle of wine, and I take her hand.

"Let's go house hunting," I say, pulling her up from the armchair.

31

There's one, tiny little Estate Agency in the village. It's run from the agent's own cosy little cottage, and if that's not the best selling point ever, I don't know what is.

This is such a surprise. I had no idea George felt the same as me in regard to our future, but it feels so good. To have someone share my dream is amazing. I don't hold out much hope that someone is selling up in the village, but maybe the next one, a further few miles away will offer us more luck.

After a brief introduction, the super-stylish, sixty-something woman in front of us cuts to the chase. She tells us that she's retiring, and relocating, to the next village, and to that end, this place is going on the market. She asks us if we would like a tour of the property.

This is all a bit uncanny. I look at George, who looks, frankly, rather strange. He keeps looking at the Estate Agent as if he, I don't know, knows her. But now he's looking straight back at me, and we both struggle to keep the smiles from our faces.

"I'll take that as a yes," she says.

It's perfect. More than perfect. Just the right balance of

modern and traditional. All fixtures and fittings will remain, so it's a no brainer. It's only going to cost seventy-five pounds more a month than we already pay. To me, that's an absolute bargain.

"So, what do you think?" George beams at me.

"I think you already know," I beam back.

We turn to the estate agent.

"Where do we sign?"

3

1

That's it. All done. Everything is unpacked, which really didn't take as long as I thought, but then when Iris has the bit between her teeth, there's no stopping her. I would have been fine with just getting in and leaving all the hard work until tomorrow, but I'm glad she persuaded me otherwise.

She's sitting across from me on the armchair, a book in her hands, and a glass of red wine on the nest of tables by her side. She looks so relaxed. This is the best day ever. Tiring, perhaps, but for all the right reasons.

"You okay?" she says, looking up with a smile.

I nod, and her eyes fall back to her book, but I don't look away. I can't take my eyes off her.

"What?" she says.

"Nothing," I sigh, "I love you."

"Love you too."

Iris is cleaning away our plates, and cutlery, the remnants of our first dinner in our new home. We've already finished off a bottle of wine, but it's Saturday night and I want to spend it in the pub across the road.

I walk up behind her and slide my hands around her waist, turn her around so I can take her all in.

"Pub?" I say.

"I thought you'd never ask," she answers as she kisses me deeply.

She throws the damp tea towel at the kitchen counter and takes me by the hand.

It's freezing tonight. I'd hasten a guess that the temperature is in the lower single figures, maybe even minus.

Iris's cheeks are flushed, a result of the brief, but blustery amble over here. She shakes off her jacket and hangs it on the coat rack in the far corner.

I order our drinks, and whilst the barman is busy pulling pints, I hang my coat up too. I pay up and take a seat opposite Iris. I watch her take a gulp of the four and a half percent craft ale and laugh as she licks the froth from her top lip.

"Oh, this is gorgeous," she says.

I take a sip of mine, and I have to agree. This could prove too easy to drink. Far too easy.

2

"Time, ladies and gents. Time please," a bearded, rosy-cheeked, rotund man bellows, even though there's only me and George in the room. Last ones standing. Or should I say sitting. It only feels a moment ago that we breezed in, but the time on the clock above the bar tells us it's eleven forty.

George grabs our coats and hands me mine. We thank the landlord and stand up. I can tell the alcohol has taken effect. Thank God we've only got to stumble back over the road.

An owl hoots somewhere in the distance, makes me jump, and then we hear the unmistakable sound of a fox baying. Welcome to the country.

3

Our new home may only be a short amble across the road, but it feels like it's taking forever. Iris is giggling like a naughty schoolgirl, slightly weaving left to right, pulling me with her.

I smile, stifling my own urge to laugh. After everything she's been through, she totally deserves this. We both do, although after everything I did, I'm still pinching myself.

I exhale deeply. Not because I'm drunk, well, maybe a little bit, but because I'm happy. So happy. I've never felt happier. I have arrived. I think we both have. This is solid, unmoving. It's forever and it's ours.

4

Our new home may only be just over the road, but it feels like it's taking forever. I know I'm drunk, but not so much that I can't feel myself swaying left to right and all over the place, for that matter. Thank God George is a bit steadier.

I smile, start to laugh. After everything I've been through, I totally deserve this. I don't care how selfish that sounds. We both deserve this. A brand-new start.

I take a deep breath, pull the crisp, wintery air into my lungs. I may be a little tipsy but hey, I'm happy. I don't think I've ever felt happier.

The one thing that would make all this perfect – Norm. He would have loved it here, the big garden, the countryside, the walks, all the walks. What's the saying? "A dog makes the house a home." I know that full well. Maybe it's time for a new one. None could ever replace him; I wouldn't want that. But it would make everything complete.

5

Ouch. My head feels like it's been trampled on by a herd of steel-toe-cap-boot wearing rhinos. I can't lift it from my pillow without seeing stars. I can feel every ounce of blood pumping through my skull. You would think that closing your eyes would alleviate it slightly. No chance.

Thing is, we probably should have gone straight to bed. It would have been the sensible thing to do, but Iris was full of the joys of spring, and alcohol, and wanted more of it. She was excited, bless her. Cracked open a bottle of Shiraz, started talking about how a "dog would make our house a home". Then we started on another.

I know she's found it hard without Norm. He was a character, that's for sure. I couldn't have said no to her even if I wanted to. I think it'll be a good thing. Our first, proper responsibility other than the mortgage. An all living, breathing, four-legged friend to take care of.

And I'll get the ball in motion. I will. Just not right now.

6

Ouch. My head feels like a herd of elephants have trampled all over it. I can barely lift it off my pillow. It hurts so much. Even closing my eyes isn't helping, not one bit. I'm staring at the back of George's head which seems to be bobbing up and down as though lost at sea.

It was my fault. We should have gone straight to bed, but I was excited, so excited that it seemed a shame not to crack open a bottle of Shiraz. It certainly made the conversation flow. Even George started getting excited. He never really had the chance to click with Norm. They just kind of tolerated each other at best, so I think it will be a good thing for both of us. Our first, proper responsibility, other than the mortgage, as a couple.

He said we should get the ball in motion, and we will. Just not right now.

7

My hangover may have abated a little, but it's given me a raging appetite, and as much as the tea and toast Iris made for us provided a much welcome satisfaction, it was short lived. If I don't get my teeth into a full English soon, I don't know what I'll do.

Thankfully, as well as learning there's a dog rescue center in the next village last night, we found out the pub is also a hotel and restaurant, and starts serving food to non-residents at ten am. The menu looked great. Not too much on there yet not too little and all-day breakfasts being served, well, all day. Mind you, they start their Sunday lunches at twelve pm. It's quarter-past eleven now. Should we wait to order a dinner, or get straight to it and do breakfast? What to do, what to do?

Iris looks like she could eat a horse and has already got her bag, and her shoes on, before I even finish asking her if she wants to go for food. We'll need the sustenance if we're going to go looking for a canine companion.

8

My hangover is just about gone, but it's given me one hell of an appetite, and as much as the tea and toast I made earlier helped, it was short lived. I want, no, need, a full English, pronto.

George doesn't have to ask me twice when he suggests we go over the road for breakfast. Then again, if we wait until twelve, we can have a proper Sunday roast. It's quarter-past eleven now. Oh my God, I can't decide. I just need food.

Whatever we have will be delicious, I'm sure, and it will give us the much-needed sustenance and energy needed to try and choose who to bring home from the rescue centre in the next village. I cannot wait.

9

The buses run a reduced service on Sundays according to the timetable. It's half past one (we waited for a dinner. It was hard to resist a full English breakfast, but we did and reaped the rewards of a roast and a couple of pints of cider) and the next bus isn't due until two-thirty. It's just under two miles to the next village.

"Shall we walk? We can work off our dinner then," Iris says, reading my mind.

It's a brighter day today, albeit rather breezy and watching Iris trying to manage her wayward locks makes me laugh. I can see how annoyed she's getting and it's so cute.

"Why didn't I tie my hair back?" she says through her teeth.

For a Sunday, the village is bustling with life. Gone are the times when the shops would close, when the last day of the week was one of rest. There's no market on, so at least tradition is being adhered to in that respect.

I can already count three pubs and we've only just turned in to it. No doubt we'll pop into one, maybe two, maybe all, on our return from the rescue centre, which we've been told is just a little further up, second right.

I feel nervous for some reason and by the look on Iris's face, I think she is too. This is going to be a big thing for us, let's not forget that. I've never had a pet before (well, I've had fish, does that count?) and certainly haven't entertained the idea of getting a dog, rescue or not, until now. There's a reason for that. It feels right, like it's fate or something.

10

The buses don't run as frequently on a Sunday and rightly so. No one should be rushing around, anywhere. Especially if you're feeling a bit squiffy as a result of a heavy night. Our Sunday dinners have gone down a treat though, so has the cider. Hair of the dog and all that.

The next bus arrives at two-thirty, an hour from now. It seems silly waiting for it when we could walk it in about half the time. I put the question to George. Walking it is. At least we can burn off the food and drink.

It's much brighter and apart from the wind blowing my hair all over the place, which is irritating the hell out of me, I feel great. Might be the hair-of-the-dog that did it, might have been the food. Either way, both have set us up for the rest of the day.

I know that Sunday isn't a day of rest anymore, but I'm still surprised at how busy the village is. People are milling around leisurely. We've already clocked a few pubs, and we've only just got here. I'm sure we'll be visiting one or all of them on the way back from the rescue centre, just to celebrate and all that.

We've been told that it's a bit further up the village, second right. I feel nervous for some reason and by the look on George's face, I think he is too. There's a reason for that. It's so much more than just getting a dog. He, or she, will be *ours*. Not mine. Not his. Ours. And it feels right, like it's fate or something.

11

As if on cue, we stop short of the door that leads to the reception. My hands feel clammy and I feel stupid for feeling so apprehensive. Iris grabs my hand, takes a deep breath.

"Okay, let's do this," she says, matter-of-factly.

I let Iris do the talking and she'll never understand how much I love seeing her like this, animated, excited, full of joy. At risk of sounding soppy, she oozes everything that's good and pure about a person.

We're asked to take a seat. There's only two other people in the room, a little girl and, I'm guessing, her Mum. The girl reminds me of Iris, well, at least her actions do. Mum is trying to calm her daughter down even though, I imagine, she's just as elated.

A scruffy little, ridiculously cute mongrel is led into the waiting room by a member of staff. The Mum and her daughter both get up from their seats, the girl clapping her hands and jumping up and down. The smile on her face seems to stretch from one ear to the other as she squeals with delight at the sight of her new friend. Her Mum quickly flicks a lone tear from her cheek, a smile playing on her lips.

Iris hasn't taken her eyes away from the pair, her smile matching the one the child wears. The Mum hugs the member of staff in thanks for the gift she has just bestowed on them. The dog has completed their family. That's how it feels to me, an onlooker.

And now, there's just us, sitting here. Waiting.

12

That was, seriously, one of the cutest things I've ever seen. If any two people ever deserved a dog, it was that little girl and her Mummy. The look of pure elation and joy on the face of the little one, and the quiet happiness in her Mother's tear-filled eyes, well, it's got me. It's taking everything in my power not to break down, to melt into a sobbing mess on the clinical smelling, linoleum floor.

I remember how I felt when I picked Norm up. I was so excited, so bloody happy, but it was tinged with sadness. It was incredibly difficult to take him away from his Mum and his brothers and sisters, to separate him from his pack. So difficult that I almost wanted to break the deal and leave him. I don't think I've ever felt so torn about anything in my life.

The door next to the reception desk opens again. I grab George's hand, squeeze it tightly. This is it.

13

Just when I think I couldn't love Iris any more than I already do, she proves me wrong. I don't know what's cuter, the brindle Bull Terrier that's straining slightly at the end of a lead, or Iris's beaming face. I don't think she could physically smile any wider. Her eyes are welling up as we stand up to greet the lady who is gently holding the dog to heel.

We're told our girl is called Jem, the name she had when she was bought in. We can change it, if we like, but we're advised she responds well to it, especially in recall training. We look at each other, silently agreeing that there'll be no change of name, that she suits it.

"She's eighteen months old and was left with us as the owner didn't realise how much hard work it would be to look after her," she continues.

Iris shakes her head in frustration and instinctively kneels. Jem's tail instantly starts to wag.

"Can I?" she asks the member of staff, itching to get her hands on our new pal.

"Of course," she replies, "she's just a bit excitable, but she's a good girl."

Iris strokes Jem's head softly and as if it knows it's okay, as if she knows that we're her new family, she loses her shit. In a good way. I bend down to get in on the action.

"She's good with kids," the lady says, "and she's fine with other dogs. She's socialised well with all the others here. We're all going to miss her. She's a proper character, and I honestly think she'll adapt to her new life, with you both, very quickly."

I take my eyes off Jem and avert them to Iris. Since we've been together, I've never seen her happier. It's contagious, magical even.

"So, what next?" I ask, allowing Iris to get even more carried away.

"We have to do a home-visit. It's a requirement and even though we have no doubt you'll love and care for Jem brilliantly," she looks down at Iris and our soon-to-be brindle beauty, "we need to make sure she's going to a good home. If we're happy with where she'll be brought up in, you can have her the same day. How does that sound?"

"Sounds perfect," Iris pipes up. It seems she's been listening all along.

"It does," I say, nodding my head.

"We can squeeze you in for a visit tomorrow, if you like?" the lady says and takes down our details.

"What time would that be? We're at work until five pm, but we could finish earlier if need be," I reply.

"If you could, or at least one of you could, we'd appreciate it. We don't do any visits after five-thirty, I'm afraid."

"Not a problem," Iris says, "if we left at four pm, we'd get back for half past, or thereabouts. Is that okay?"

"That's brilliant, thank you. We'll aim to be with you by half past four, then. If you're struggling, just let reception know and they'll notify me."

"Not a problem. Thank you for fitting us in so quickly," I tell her.

"My pleasure. In the meantime, would you like to take Jem out for a walk? See how you feel with her on the lead?"

"Yes please," Iris answers, childlike.

We're directed back through the door behind reception and told that we'll be let out onto a field out back.

I let Iris do the honours and watch her eyes close in delight as she takes the lead.

14

Just when I think I couldn't be happier, I'm proved wrong. We've only just met Jem (that's her name) and I'm in love already. Her markings are gorgeous; dark brown-red brindle all over and a white, left paw. She's beautiful.

My happiness dwindles slightly as Jem's carer tells us the reason she was bought in to the centre. It's so frustrating and makes me so angry. Why have a pet if you can't look after it? It sickens me. Then again, their loss is our gain.

She's doing the same little happy dance that Norm used to do when he used to greet me, and any bad thoughts are banished.

A home visit has been arranged for tomorrow, after work and if everything meets requirements, Jem will stay with us. We've got to make sure we can leave early, but I don't think it'll be too much of an issue.

And now, I'm holding her lead and we're being directed out back to take our new dog on our first walk together.

LUCY ONIONS

15

The champagne may be a touch on the expensive side, but it feels right. This is a celebration. It's not just because of Jem, it's everything. It's because I'm ecstatic and I want to treat us both to a little luxury. We deserve it.

The pub is cosy and warm, welcoming. I don't think they sell much champagne in here, or at least that's the feeling I'm getting from the barman. He looks shocked at the request, but I can also imagine the pound signs rolling over in his head like he's just taken a turn on a one-armed bandit.

Iris smiles as I head back to our table with the ice-bucket, bottle nestled between the cubes, and two glasses.

"Do you think it might be too early to celebrate?" she says, "I mean, we don't know we've definitely got her yet."

"Now, Iris," I say, easing the cork until it pops gently, "tomorrow is just a formality, just going through the motions. They've got to do the home-visit, but we've got this. We've got Jem. I'd bet on it."

"You're right, I suppose. They seemed really happy we were there."

"They were. I almost felt like they wanted us to take her today, but they've got to do things by the book. Imagine the trouble they would be in if they were found out."

"Once again, George, you are correct."

I fill our flutes slowly, careful not to let the fizzy liquid spill over on to the table. That would be a terrible waste. I hand one to Iris and smile as she takes a sip.

"It's happening," she giggles, "it's really happening."

"I know."

She puts her glass on the table and pulls her chair close to mine. Any closer and she would be on my lap. She takes my hands into hers and leans in.

"I love you so much, George," she whispers.

16

The champagne is a nice touch, albeit an expensive one, but it feels right. This is a celebration. It's not just because of Jem, it's everything. It's about everything we've been through to get here. We deserve this.

I smile as I watch George head back to our table with the ice-bucket, bottle and two glasses.

"Do you think it might be too early to celebrate?" I ask, "I mean, we don't know we've definitely got her yet."

"Now, Iris," he says, gently popping the cork, "tomorrow is just a formality, just going through the motions. They've got to do the home-visit, but we've got this. We've got Jem. I'd bet on it."

"You're right, I suppose," I say, "They seemed really happy we were there."

"They were. I almost felt like they wanted us to take her today, but they've got to do things by the book. Imagine the trouble they would be in if they were found out."

"Once again, George, you are correct."

He fills our glasses carefully. We shouldn't waste a drop at this price. He hands me one of the flutes and I take a sip. I can't stop the smile that emerges.

"It's happening. It's really happening."

"I know," he says, smiling back at me.

I put my glass on the table. I've got to get closer to him. If we weren't in public, I'd be on his lap now but we are, so I take his hands in mine and tell him that I love him. And I do so love him.

17

The bubbles seem to have taken effect on Iris. She can't be drunk, can she? We only had one bottle between us and that's hardly enough to get tipsy on, but she's giddy with something, that's for sure. Maybe it's the mixture of alcohol and excitement that's causing it. Whatever it is that's resulted in her behavior right now, I like it. If we wouldn't have been in view of anyone in the pub, I'm sure she would have been all over me like a rash. When I suggested we head home, she didn't put up any kind of fight.

It's quiet out now even though it's only just gone seven. The pubs are still open, but they don't look anywhere near as busy as they did when we first got here. It's been an eventful day and I'm tired. The same cannot be said for Iris. She's buzzing and I'm certain, if we hadn't got work tomorrow, this evening would not be ending any time soon.

As we turn on to the road that will lead us back home, the sun is starting to set over the moors and the colours filling the sky are stunning. From this vantage point, it's easy to see our little village. I don't think I'll ever tire of the views here. If there's a heaven, I've no doubt it'll look something like this.

Iris sighs happily.

"Beautiful, isn't it?" she says.

18

The bubbles seem to have gone to my head a little bit. I can't be drunk, can I? We only had one bottle between us. I mean, it's nothing is it? Maybe it's the mixture of alcohol and excitement that's causing it.

It took everything in my power to behave in the pub. I wanted George there and then, but I don't think that would have gone down well with the punters looking on. When George suggested we head home, I wasn't about to refuse.

It's only just gone seven and although the pubs are still open, they're nowhere near as busy as they were earlier. George seems tired, but I'm far from it. If we hadn't got work tomorrow, I don't think we'd be on our way home. Well, not yet.

We turn on to the road that takes us back home. The sun is just beginning to set, and the sky is stunning. Its colours are staining the moors below it with hues of reds, oranges and yellows. From here, it's easy to see our lovely little village. I don't think I'll ever tire of these views. If there's a heaven, this is what it must look like.

"Beautiful, isn't it?" I say, breathing in the air around me.

"It is," George sighs back

19

This is why I don't drink champagne often. I love the taste and how happy and relaxed it makes me feel, but I don't love the bad head I get as a result. It's like someone is in there, pummeling a bass drum.

I get up, steadying myself as the room spins a little. My mouth tastes like something's crawled inside and died and the only thought in my head is to get to the bathroom. I need painkillers and toothpaste. In my inebriated haste to get to the bathroom, my brain forgets that there's a solid oak door on the way there and promptly, painfully, I stub my left, little toe. The most incredible pain shoots through my body and I'm sorry, but there's nothing I can do to stop the utter filth that flies from my mouth. I even say the *worst* word. Iris hates it. She's going to fucking kill me.

"Toast or cereal?" she calls from the landing.

"Fuck. Toast," I shout, immediately realising how ridiculous I sound.

"I didn't know that was a *thing* – fucking toast?" she giggles. Her footsteps are quick down the stairs.

The toaster pops just as I step into the kitchen. Coffee's ready too by the smell of it.

"Oh, hey," Iris greets me. She's dying to laugh, I can tell.

"Hey," I say, pecking her cheek.

"You okay?"

"Just remind me to open my eyes when I get out of bed next time," I laugh.

We're not in the old place anymore. We literally could have walked around it with our eyes closed. Everything was pretty much in reaching distance, all amenities just a step or two away. That's how it felt anyway. This is a house. With an upstairs and a downstairs. And space. Lots of it.

We eat our breakfast and wash and change quickly.

I unlock the front door, take a deep breath and look at Iris.

"I am so excited," I tell her.

I'm not the only one.

20

This is why I don't drink champagne often. I love the taste of it and how giggly it makes me, but I don't love what it does to my head the morning after. But even though it feels like there's a little dude in my head pounding a big bass drum, I'm feeling optimistic.

I open the bathroom cabinet, pull out a pack of ibuprofen, throw a couple in my mouth and drink straight from the tap. The cold water makes my teeth ache, but it's refreshing, and I gulp greedily.

George is stirring, sounding more like a bear with a sore head than a human being. There's a loud thud and the words coming from his mouth are nothing short of pure filth.

"Toast or cereal?" I ask. It's going to have to be a quick breakfast this morning.

"Fuck. Toast," he shouts.

"I didn't know that was a *thing* – fucking toast?" I giggle and immediately realise I may have said the wrong thing. I quickly take to the stairs, doing my best to hold in laughter.

I put the coffee pot on and drop four slices of bread into the toaster. I take a pen from the knife and fork drawer, which, you know, is where everyone keeps their stash and rip a page from my to-do list pad, and make a note of what we need to pick up after work, before our home visit later.

I mean, I suppose I could just put Norm's old stuff out, his bed and his toys and whatnot, but Jem is new, our girl, and she deserves new things. She can put her own scent on everything then, mark her territory.

The toaster pops and our coffee is ready, just in time it seems.

"Oh, hey," I greet George, fighting back a smile.

"Hey," he says and pecks my cheek.

"You okay?"

"Just remind me to open my eyes when I get out of bed next time," he laughs.

It's right though. We were so used to the old place that we literally could have walked around it with our eyes closed. Everything was pretty much in reaching distance, all amenities just a few steps away. That's how it felt anyway. This is a house. With an upstairs and a downstairs. And space. Lots of it.

It doesn't feel like we've eaten our breakfast. I'd go so far as to say we just inhaled it. We both wash and change quickly and head back downstairs.

George unlocks the front door and stops, looks at me, takes a deep breath.

"I am so excited," he says.

He's not the only one.

21

I'm trying, I really am, but the mix of excitement about seeing Jem and the last remnants of a hangover have done a good job on me. I've clock-watched all day and I'll be bloody glad to get out of here.

I've barely got through a few submissions and to be honest, I'll be going back through them again tomorrow because I know I haven't given them my full attention. Thankfully, the boss is on holiday this week, so there's no one breathing down our necks.

It doesn't help that Iris seems as agitated as me. She's done nothing but fidget and fuss, over what, I can't see. All I know is that I've never seen her drink so much coffee.

It's three-forty-five. We need to leave at four at the latest so that we're back home in time. I'm apprehensive, nervous and so bloody excited.

I start to pack up, images of the three of us dancing through my head. I look over at Iris. Her smile matches mine. By the end of the night, we'll be a family. Well, as close to one as we'll get without having a baby. We both stand to leave, our smiles growing wider by the second.

22

I'm trying, I really am, but the mix of excitement at welcoming Jem into our home and the remnants of a hangover have really clouded my productivity. And if I look at the clock once more, I might just scream. It feels like every minute has lasted an hour.

I've just about managed to get through two submissions. Two out of six. That is not good. Luckily the boss is out of office this week so there's no one breathing down our necks. But I'm angry with myself. The less I do today means more for the rest of the week and I just, urgh.

It doesn't help that George is as agitated as me. He's been up and down like a yo-yo all day. I've never seen him drink so much coffee.

The digital clock on the bottom, right-hand corner of my screen reads three-forty-five. We need to leave at four at the latest so that we're back home in time.

I start to pack up, my heart beating a little faster than usual. Images of us - me, George and Jem - fly around my head. I look over at George. His smile matches mine. By the end of the night, we'll be a family. Well, as close to one as we'll get without having a baby. We both stand to leave, our smiles growing wider by the second.

LUCY ONIONS

23

"Well, that's it then. She's all yours," Katie says, an audible wobble in her voice, "I'm going to miss this one. She's a one off, that's for sure. I was this close to keeping her, but then I say that about all of them."

"We can't thank you, and all the staff at the center enough," Iris tells her, hoping to make the separation a little easier, "it's clear you've taken excellent care of her."

"They've just got such a bad rep and it's not warranted. If I didn't have two already, I would have snapped this little girl up when she first came to us, but I'm so happy she's coming to you. I mean look at her? I think she's in love already."

Jem is smiling. I mean actually, properly smiling. Her tail is wagging, hitting the side of the sofa with such force, it sounds like a bass drum.

"So, any issues or problems, just let us know," Katie goes on, "but I honestly don't think you'll get any, other than, maybe, a few unsettled days and nights. She's used to being surrounded by her pals, and the bloody noises they make. Just give her time and she'll be your best friend ever. I'm certain of it."

My thoughts turn to Norm, and how he and Iris were best friends. He was a one off, a real character, but I think she's ready now. Ready for a new, best friend. Ready to love another crazy dog.

I can feel a lump forming in my throat and I do my best to swallow it down and keep the tears at bay. All Katie needs now is for us to start crying.

24

I struggle to hold it together as Katie walks down our front path towards her car. She doesn't turn around and look back, but I can see from her body language, by the way her head has dropped, and how her shoulders are slowly, softly shaking, that looking back would be the worst thing she could do right now. I've never been through this before. It's so fucking sad, but at the same time, I'm so happy.

I look to my right and smile as George waves and shouts goodbye to someone who's not going to answer, and then I look down at Jem, sitting patiently between us. I don't speak dog, but her happy little face and eyes follow Katie all the way down the drive. She cocks her head, right to left, and her tail isn't wagging anymore.

Katie's car door shuts. She reverses slightly, rights herself, and drives off into the sunset to the sound of Jem's cries.

LUCY ONIONS

25

I couldn't do it, work in a rescue center. I'd be a wreck. I take my hat off to anyone who can. It breaks my heart watching Katie walk away. It's easy to see how much she loves Jem. She keeps straight, doesn't look back, not even when she gets in her car.

I wave and call goodbye to her, but I don't expect a response. I know I wouldn't be able to. And then I look down at Jem, sitting patiently between us. She watches Katie all the way back to her car and her tail stops wagging the moment she drives away.

All that's left is the sound of a revving engine and Jem's cries.

4

1

The problem with living literally a hop, skip and a jump away from your local pub is trying to resist the urge to frequent it on a nightly basis. It's a proper, country pub with a multitude of guest ales and ciders. It's got its own micro-brewery out back and they make their own gin in the basement.

I'm a big fan of the gin, especially when it's paired with a good quality mixer, and accompanied by a bit of fruit. Peppercorns are nice in gin too. Never thought I'd ever drink a drink with pepper in, but then again, I never thought I'd get into gin and tonic or "posh drinks". That's what I used to call them. I couldn't be doing with all that nonsense before we moved here. I still love my wine, and enjoy a beer or two, but they don't seem to refresh me. I tend to only drink a nice red at home now, or when we're here, enjoying a nice meal. I can't drink gin with a meal. Oh no. That wouldn't be right.

Jem's a fan too (not of the gin, obviously), especially if there's a bag of pork scratchings involved. George always says they're for her, but I think that's just a ruse.

If it was up to me, we'd have dinner here every evening too, but we'd end up going bankrupt.

I put a joint of pork in the slow cooker before we came over and it just so happens, we've got another hour before it's finished.

"One for the road?" George asks.

He hasn't got to ask me twice.

Jem just snores some more.

She's fit in so well with us, and she's honestly been no trouble at all. Everyone seems to love her. Well, everyone in the pub anyway. I'm totally in love with her, and since I've dropped a couple of days at work, I've been able to spend more time training her, and just being with her more. I couldn't be happier. I've always been a bit of a homebody, but it's not because of that. I've started my own publishing imprint. It's always been my dream and now that dream has come true.

George helps me with formatting any manuscripts that are sent to in (it's definitely his forte), but everything else I do myself. I love it.

I look out of the window at our home. This is how our life was always meant to be. We were made for this.

2

The problem with living literally a hop, skip and a jump away from your local pub is trying to resist the urge to frequent it on a nightly basis. I should just give up. Give in to the urge. It's not a pub that you rock up in for an all-nighter. It's a proper, country pub with guest ales and ciders galore. It's got its own micro-brewery out back and they make their own gin in the basement. Iris is a big fan of the gin, particularly if it's a double, accompanied by a fancy tonic mixer, in one of those fish-bowl glasses with a shit load of fruit or peppercorns, or even sprigs of rosemary, in it. I mean, what the fuck? Rosemary? That's all a bit too much for me. How the hell are you supposed to drink with all that faff in the way?

I never thought I'd see Iris drink a "posh" drink. That's what she used to call them. She used to say, "No, none of that nonsense for me." She still enjoys a beer or two and is more than partial to a nice red wine at home, but it's like she's discovered fire with this new taste for a distilled spirit.

Jem's a fan too (not of the gin, obviously), especially if there's a bag of pork scratchings involved. I always say they're for her, but man, they are beautiful, so most of the time, it's me that crunches through the lion's share of them.

If it was up to me, we'd have dinner here every evening too, but funds won't permit that unfortunately.

Before we ambled over, Iris put a joint of pork in the slow cooker. She's smothered it in wholegrain mustard, apple sauce and poured in a little stock and white wine. She put it on low for six hours. I'm surprised we can't smell it from here.

We've got another hour before it's finished making our home smell amazing.

"One for the road?" I ask her.

"You haven't got to ask me twice," she replies.

Jem just snores some more.

She's fit in so well with us, with the community (by that I mean everyone in the pub) and she's honestly been no trouble at all. Iris is totally in love with her, and since she dropped a couple of days at work, she's a different woman. She's happier. She's always been a bit of a homebody, I can attest to that, but now, she's just come into her own. Let me be clear, she's not a housewife. Well, she doesn't like to be called one, at least. She just enjoys it, this, our life.

The reason we could afford her going part time – well, she's started her own publishing imprint. It's always been her dream and now that dream has come true. She's worked bloody hard for it too.

I help her with formatting any manuscripts that are sent to her (that's my thing, to be honest), but everything else she does herself. She loves it, and I love her for loving it. I love how she chews at pens and pushes her glasses up her nose when they've slid a little too far down.

I head to the bar, call the round in. No more pork-based treats for little miss Jem though, she'll stink the pub out.

I look back at Iris. She's stroking Jem's head and smiling, looking out of the window at our home. This is how our life was meant to be. We were made for this.

3

There's a look in George's eyes and I understand it completely. Just the thought of what's in store makes me shiver, gives me goosebumps. I can feel my cheeks burning and I don't think it's just the alcohol that has caused the reaction.

Have you ever tried to, you know, do stuff, when you've got a dog who thinks the only thing you can love is them? It takes a fair bit of bribery and good, solid doors.

Without speaking, we finish our drinks and put our coats on. George gestures for me to go in front, which is inevitable anyway what with Jem pulling at her lead. She has to be in front, this dog. As I pass by him, he slaps my behind playfully.

It's on!

4

I look at Iris and I wonder if she's picking up the signal. The ones that says, "I want you. Now. Right now." Obviously, I tell my brain, we can't do it here. Let's just wait until we get home.

She's got hardly any make up on, and to be honest, if there's anyone who doesn't need an ounce of it, it's her. My brain is whirring with what I want to do with her. Just the thought of what's in store makes me shiver, gives me goosebumps. I can feel my cheeks burning and I don't think it's completely down to the alcohol.

Have you ever tried to, you know, get it on, when you've got a dog? It's all about bribery, good timing, and remembering to shut your bedroom door.

We finish our drinks and put our coats on. I gesture to Iris to go in front (she's got no choice anyway what with Jem pulling at her lead. She has to be in front, this dog!). As she passes me, I slap her behind playfully.

It's on!

LUCY ONIONS

5

The wind has really picked up, and we're literally having to hold on to each other as if our lives depend on it. Jem is not a fan of extreme weather conditions. High winds freak her out, and the rain, well, taking her a walk is nigh on impossible.

We cross the road, or should I say we're pulled there, and I can't wait to get inside. I let Jem off her lead, and she takes no time in getting to the front door. She sits there shaking. If she could talk, I'm sure she would be telling us to hurry up.

George pulls the key from his pocket and slips it into the lock, steals a kiss as he opens the door.

We practically fall into the house, excitedly pulling at our coats, desperate to get them off.

He pulls me to his chest, wraps his arms around me. I love how I feel in them; safe, secure. He puts his lips on mine and we kiss with urgency.

Jem jumps up my leg, letting us know that she's still in the room. I steal away from the kiss and look down at her.

"Come on, Jem. Give us a break," I tell her.

And then I spot it, and any thoughts of romance are swiftly quelled.

LUCY ONIONS

6

It's as if Iris is opening the envelope in slow motion. Her hands are trembling, her face as white as the paper she's fumbling with. Tears fill her staring, wide eyes as she hands it to me. Jem is sitting, looking up at her, cocking her head from side to side, eyes full of concern.

"It's for you, again," she says, eager to let go of it.

I take it from her but don't look down, I don't look anywhere else but at her eyes.

Iris is pacing, biting her nails, struggling to hold it together.

"Well?" she says, "Read it."

What if I don't want to? Reading it, especially out loud, will mean it's real. I don't want it to be. I gulp, my mouth suddenly dry.

"For fuck sake!" Iris shouts, scaring Jem in the process. She kneels down to comfort her, tells her she's sorry.

"I thought this was all done with," she cries.

I thought the same too. I honestly believed that moving away would put a stop to it for good.

I dish up our dinner to give me something to do. A

distraction more than anything else. I can see, just by the look on her face, and her body language, that food isn't high up on her list of priorities. I'm not so sure I want to eat myself. Not right now.

Jem, on the other hand, is looking at me as if she's never been fed. At least someone in the house will benefit from what's been bubbling away all day.

Iris believed that the last letter I received was from someone from work. I didn't disagree with her, but just couldn't see who would ever do that. But now, I'm starting to see why she would think that. She's got to be right. She must be. I don't know anyone outside of work, well apart from the landlord and staff at the pub, a few of the regulars, and the family in the cottage at the top of the hill, and even at work, there's only Adam and Lucas, my former best friends. We were so close, the three of us. I loved those guys like brothers. I loved being in the band.

If I wouldn't have been playing that night, I would never have approached Iris. I'd probably still be writing those letters now, still making her life a misery.

Everything changed though, with me and them. Changed when I got together with Iris. Adam isn't right with me, not at all. Neither is Lucas, to be honest, but Adam, he's really taken it badly. I wish I knew what it is I've done to hurt him.

No. It can't be him. He wouldn't have broken into Iris's, would he? He wouldn't have followed us here, just to leave this, would he?

7

This is just unbelievable. We'd put the letters behind us. I mean, we'll never forget how they made us feel, what they did to us, but we got through it and we've become stronger as a result. But, once again, our peace has been broken, ruined.

And it's not George's fault, not at all, so why am I being so standoffish with him? Whoever left that last letter in the loft, whoever creeped into our bedroom and put the other in my dressing gown pocket, and I've got a damn good idea who did, broke in. How am I supposed to feel safe now? They didn't just break into my property, they broke into my mind, left me feeling the least confident I've ever felt.

And it's not George's fault. Or is it? He's got more than enough experience in writing letters and creeping around to make sure I got them. Maybe he's the culprit? Back to his old tricks again, writing letters to himself to act as a smokescreen, to cover his back?

He dishes up two lots of our slow-cooked pork. I don't know why. I'm not hungry. In fact, the last thing on my mind right now is food. But that's okay, because there's a four-legged-friend ready and waiting for whatever she can get.

George sidles up to me, circling his arm around my

shoulders. I recoil, wriggle from his grasp. I cannot believe how shitty I'm being to him, but I can't help it, and I hate myself for it.

"Hey," he says, despairingly. The sound of his voice makes my heart ache, but I need to be away from him right now because I don't want to tell him exactly what's in my head.

"I'm tired. Good night," I say bluntly, heading for the stairs. There's truth in it though. I'm exhausted, mentally and physically.

"Okay," he sighs.

I hate myself.

8

Why is she being so…like this? What the hell am I supposed to have done wrong? I get that this is all a bit of history repeating, but this time, along with the last, it's nothing to do with me. Maybe she's just taking shit out on me because I'm the only person she can do that with. It hurts though, really fucking hurts. She may have said goodnight, but she certainly doesn't mean it.

I'm not staying down here any longer. I've given her some alone time, time to think through her shit, but that's it. I can't lie, I'm angry. The hurt has gone, well, no, it's still there, but it's been pushed to one side, like I've been.

She can't treat me this way. She needs to get over herself and realise that we're a partnership now. When she hurts, so do I. She can't flip me off like I'm nothing.

Jem is sitting at the bottom of the stairs. She's torn. Should she go up to Iris or stay with me? I pat my leg and tell her to come. She doesn't need telling twice.

I open our bedroom door and find her sitting on our bed, breaking her heart. Jem jumps straight up next to her, puts her head on her lap.

Iris looks up at me with raw, red, bloodshot eyes, and it cripples me.

"I'm so sorry," she sobs, her voice shaking in time with her shoulders, "I'm being such a bitch. Please forgive me."

I cross the room in three strides and sit down beside her, pull her into me, envelope her in my arms. I tell her she doesn't need to be sorry, whisper the words into her hair. I was ready to go in there, all guns blazing. I was going to tell her how much she'd hurt me, how angry she'd made me feel, but I believe her. I know she's sorry.

"There's nothing to forgive," I sigh.

"There is, and I am. I'm really sorry."

We stare at each other. A silent agreement is made. We need to remove Jem from this particular equation. For all of our sakes.

"Come on," I tell her, once again tapping my leg. She looks at me with those sad eyes, and I instantly feel guilty. But not for long.

She takes the hint eventually, does as she's told, but her eyes never leave me, even as I shut the door on her.

I sit back beside Iris and lean in. She does too. Our noses are a hair's breadth apart. Iris takes the lead, kisses me like it's the last time we ever will. She forces me backwards. I do nothing to stop her. She climbs over me, her knees sinking into the bed either side of my hips. Her eyes are full of intensity, of need, and I don't think she's ever looked like this to me before, so dangerously sexy.

She bends at the hip, lowering the top half of her body, close enough that I can feel her shortened breath tickling my mouth.

I dare not do exactly what I want to, lean up to her and take her full, plump lips into my mouth. I dare not take the bottom one between my teeth. I dare not kiss her so hard she struggles for air or flip her over and have my way. This is her show. She's the conductor, and I am merely her player.

9

I can't take my eyes off him. I'm mesmerised by the rise and fall of his chest, his nostrils flaring ever so slightly, by his eyes flitting around beneath his eyelids. I wonder what he's dreaming of.

I hope he'll forgive me. I can't believe how vile I've been. I should know better, should know that this is affecting him just as much as me.

I scoot around his dormant form, trying my very best not to wake him. I throw my dressing gown on and slide my feet into slippers. I open the bedroom door slowly, glancing behind me, checking he's still deep in sleep.

I head downstairs and load up the coffee percolator with enough ground beans and water to keep us caffeinated until at least lunchtime. I pick up my book, settle into the armchair and sigh. This is perfect, and there's no way I'm going to let some silly letter spoil this.

10

I'm ravenous, and as I step out of the bedroom, I smell coffee and bacon. Heaven.

The dining table is set, and it takes every ounce of restraint in me not to run to it, sit down and hold my knife and fork, like a child, in readiness.

Jem is sitting beside me, crying quietly, waiting for any scrap of food that might make it towards her salivating mouth.

Iris doesn't seem to have heard me come down, which is most likely due to the fact she's singing along to Gold Dust Woman by Fleetwood Mac. She's completely oblivious to my presence, so I creep up behind her. I stand still, struggling to hold in my impending giggle. She stops singing, spins around.

"Jesus!" she shouts.

"Sorry, I couldn't resist."

"You nearly gave me a heart attack!"

I laugh heartily.

"Oh, funny is it?" she says, trying, but failing, to sound serious.

"Kind of," I say and pull her into me.

"I'm glad to hear that your girlfriends... decline... in health... is a... laughing... matter," she says between kisses.

I don't answer but take the kiss up a notch.

She breathlessly breaks away.

"Let's eat."

"Shall we go for a walk?" I ask, feeling like I'm about to pop.

"Um."

"It's no problem. If you don't fancy it. I don't mind."

"I was going to try and finish my book," she says, "I wasn't going to set foot anywhere today."

"It's cool, honest. Do you mind if I go anyway?"

"Of course not," she says, clearly relieved, "are you sure you don't mind me staying here?""

"Not at all. Might do us both a bit of good."

"You coming?" I ask Jem, and if dogs could speak, she'd be saying, "I think I'll leave it, thank you."

Iris gets up from her chair and heads round to me, plants a kiss on my forehead.

I get up, get washed and changed, ready to step out into the cold, country air.

11

I get the log fire going even though the heating is working just fine on its own. Jem circles, and then settles, into her favourite spot in front of it. If you could see bliss, give that word an image, this would be it.

I light all five of my scented candles, three on the bay windowsill, two on the hearth. I didn't tell George a time to be back for even though he asked. I'll just dish his dinner up, and he can eat whenever he wants.

This feels nice. It feels good to have some time apart. It's necessary if you want to keep a hold of your sanity, and after what happened last night, we were both very close to losing it.

I've poured myself a rather large glass of Malbec and I'm determined to finish the rest of this book today. I want to move on to another. I'm quietly hoping that George stays out for quite a while.

The pub kicked out half an hour ago now, and the only light permeating the almost pitch-black darkness, is from the street lantern at the end of our driveway, and the few illuminated windows at the pub.

No sign of George. I know we didn't agree on a time, but

I'm worried.

I've tried his phone. It's dead.

Where is he?

12

I'm starting to come round, but fuck, the right side of my head feels like it's been smashed with a sledgehammer. I can hear myself mumbling, murmuring. I know what I want to say but my mouth won't form the words. I'm fighting with my eyelids. I need them open.

A room comes slowly into view, but it's not one of ours. My head feels like it's going to explode now, and my vision is blurred. The room is spinning, but this is no hangover.

Shit! My hands are behind my back and my wrists are sore. What the fuck? I'm tied up. Not just my hands, I realise, but my ankles too. I know why I'm mumbling, why my mouth won't let me speak. This isn't a case of chronic cottonmouth.

I can hear my blood pumping, and with each second, panic is setting well and truly in.

There's a giggle, cheeky and childlike. I crane my neck, turn my head to the direction it's coming from.

13

This is so not George. I don't want to be over possessive. I don't need him to constantly check in with me. I don't want him to feel like he has to. But the pub is just there, across the road, and this is not right.

I've got visions of terrible things flying around my head. I'm not going to say them out loud. They're bad enough as it is.

Even Jem is concerned. She's pacing up and down. She's not settling.

She doesn't like this.

I don't like this.

14

Adam is sitting, front to back, on a wooden chair. Staring. Smiling. Freaking the shit out of me. My head feels just slightly less painful, and if I was able, I'd beat the living daylights out of him right now.

He gets up from the chair and kicks it to the side. He walks slowly towards me, a strange look on his face. I know that look, I've seen it before, but never from a man, especially not this one. It's the look I get from Iris when she feels, well, you know?

"Adam?" I ask nervously.

He laughs, smiles.

He kneels down in front of me, and I recoil, turn my face away as he strokes it. He grabs my chin and jerks my head back, holds it in place. He inches his face towards mine, closer and closer. I shut my eyes, repulsed and terrified.

I feel his tongue on my cheek and he licks. What the fuck?

"Open your eyes, George," he says, "Look at me."

I can't.

I don't want to.

I won't.

"Open them," his voice drops, deep, guttural and low.

No!

He slaps my face hard and I taste my blood.

"You're really going to want to do as I say, George. It'll be better if you do."

I let my eyelids open slowly, and all I can see is his face. My eyes are full of him.

"That's better," he smiles.

I'm terrified.

He knows.

"Please don't tell me you're scared of your best friend?"

What can I say?

I shake my head.

"You are!" he laughs, "Come on, George. It's just me."

I find my voice.

"Adam, what's going on? Why are you doing this?"

"Doing what?"

"This. All this," I say, shaking my tied hands at him.

"It's the only way, George."

"For what? To what?"

"To talk to you."

"What?"

"To be with you."

My stomach flips.

"If you wanted to talk to me, why didn't you just ask?"

"I don't know whether you've noticed, but since you've been with Iris, you've pushed me, and Lucas, to one side. You don't give us the time of day anymore."

"Oh, come on, Adam! Seriously?"

"Oh yes. Totally."

"She's my girlfriend. That's kind of what happens. You spend most of your time with them."

"It doesn't mean you have to shut us out, shut me out!"

"I'm sorry you feel that way, but, well, what can I say?"

"We may as well be complete strangers, George. You never want to do anything with me. You don't want to go out. We used to be so close, you and me. We used to do pretty much everything together."

"Jesus, Adam! We were in a band…"

"Were?" he shouts, "So, are we done?"

"I don't know, are we?"

Adam closes his eyes, shakes his head.

"It's her," he mumbles, "she's done this to us."

"Us? What the hell's got into you? We're friends. That's all."

"No!" he bellows, "That's not just all we are. You know what we have, what we had, is more than that."

"You're fucking crazy!"

He slaps me again. The sting brings tears to my eyes.

"How dare you! How dare you act like we're nothing more than friends."

"When have I ever given you any doubt of that?"

"You horrible, horrible man."

There are tears in his eyes now, and as he blinks, they fall down his cheeks.

"All those times you stayed with me. All those late nights, after gigs, when we crashed out together on the sofa. All those nights you told me you loved me. You're telling me it all means nothing?"

"Bloody hell, Adam. That's what friends do! I did love you, but as a friend, nothing more. You're reading way too much into it."

"You kissed me. After our first ever gig. You waited until Lucas went home, and you kissed me."

"I was drunk, Adam. High on atmosphere and beer. And I wasn't aware I'd "waited" for Lucas to go home.

"But you did."

"Maybe so."

"And you can't have been that drunk because you wouldn't have…"

"Text you to apologise?" I finish his sentence.

"Yes."

"I text you because I felt awful for it."

"It didn't feel awful," he says, voice full of disappointment. God, I feel bad for him now.

"It wasn't awful. I didn't mean it like that. It was wrong of me and that's why I apologised."

"It wasn't wrong. You know it. It was you who kissed me, and it didn't exactly look like you hated it."

I can't disagree with him. I didn't hate it, but that doesn't mean there was anything in it.

"I got caught up in the moment, that's all. That's all it was, and all it will ever be."

He takes a deep breath, composes himself, cups my face in his hands. His eyes bore into mine.

"Do you know how much I hate you right now?" he says, leaning in, his lips mere millimeters from mine.

I brace myself.

"I can guess," I say through gritted teeth, "and I'm sorry. I'm so sorry."

"You will be."

15

I can't sleep. Don't want to. It's three thirty am and George still isn't home. Jem has calmed down enough to sleep, so calm, in fact, that it would probably take a natural disaster to wake her.

Oh, to have no worries.

Oh, to be a dog.

I should phone the police. I should phone them and tell them that this is not like him. Not like him at all.

But I know what they'll say, or at least, I think I do. They'll say he's probably had too much to drink, that he's sleeping it off somewhere. They might be right. Maybe he did go into town, maybe he wanted to carry on, to enjoy himself that little bit more.

Maybe he didn't even go to the pub. He didn't say he was. He could be lying in a ditch somewhere. He could be injured, or... No, I can't think that. I must stop thinking that.

He's just letting his hair down.

If he's not back in the morning, oh wait, it already is.

16

"Come on, let's go," Adam says, dragging me up and out of his garage.

"Where?"

"Oh, it's a surprise," he laughs.

It's dusk and the street is silent apart from the sound of the birds beginning their morning chorus. I look at my watch. Three thirty am.

"Adam, why am I here? How did I get here?"

"Let's just hurry up, huh? I'm taking you back home."

I exhale, relief filling me.

"I expect Iris will be worried."

"She will be, yes."

"I don't know why she loves you so much, why she's even still with you. Maybe it's fear."

He shoves me into the passenger side of his car. I'd do just about anything to punch his lights out.

"What the hell do you mean?"

"Oh, come on," he snorts, pulling his seatbelt over his shoulder, "after what you did, you're lucky she even gives you the time of day. Like I say, I think she's only with you because she's scared of what would happen if she wasn't."

"You're talking bullshit, Adam. I don't know what the

hell…"

"I know what you did, what you were doing. I know about the letters you were sending her. I know you were stalking her. It's sick, cowardly, and it's the only way you'd ever get a girlfriend. You've scared her into this sham of a relationship."

And that makes me wonder.

17

The knock on the door is fast, fervent, impatient. I sigh and feel relief flood through me. All at once, I want to kiss George, suffocate him with them, and shout and scream at him.

Jem launches off the bed, shooting down my theory that it would take a natural disaster to rouse her.

I catch a quick glimpse of myself in the mirror, halfway down the stairs. I look like I haven't slept for a week. The bags under my eyes have bags of their own. This is what love is. All or nothing. For better or worse.

I open the front door and scream. I feel like I'm going to pass out. I know it's George, just about. I know it's his face I'm looking at underneath the blood and bruises. I can barely see his eyes, such is the extent of the swelling surrounding them. He looks broken and scared, and it's breaking my heart.

I pull him to my chest, but he doesn't relax, not even a little bit. He's rigid, frozen in fear. I close my eyes against the tears that are filling them.

And then there's a sound.

A cough.

I open my blurred, watery eyes to see Adam standing in the open doorway. I push George to one side and launch myself at Adam, fists tight, ready for action. But he's quicker than me, and I don't see his hand coming towards my face.

The pain starts in my right cheek, and quickly radiates. My vision doubles, flickers and fades to black.

It's the smell that wakes me, sending urgent signals to my brain. It's an unmistakable aroma, the smell of petrol.

My head hurts so much. It's a mixture of dull ache and searing pain, but I must fight it.

There are two dining table chairs, right in the middle of the lounge. George sits on one of them, tied up, black tape covering his mouth.

I can hear Jem's muffled barking. She's been locked away somewhere, by the sound of it. I hope to God she's not hurt.

I'm being lifted. Adam's hands hurt my armpits. He dumps me on the chair next to George, and I instantly reach out to my boyfriend. I've got to make the most of this time, got to touch him, feel him, just in case it's the last thing I do.

George's eyes are full of tears. He shakes his head and looks at Adam, who is now standing in front of me, tape in hands, ready to silence me. But he's not tied my hands, not secured me to the chair. There's hope. There's still that.

I shout at Adam, tell him to let us go. He just laughs.

"Whatever it is you think you're doing; you will not get away with it," I scream.

"If I can't have him, neither will you."

Adam sticks tape over my mouth, and then pulls cable ties from his pocket, smiles and waves them in my face.

I really try not to let him know that he's pulled the ties too tight, but I can't stop the muffled scream of pain that escapes me.

18

It's no use. I just can't get myself free. He's done a good job on the bindings. Every time I try to move, it feels like they're getting even tighter. I really would give anything to destroy him, right now. I'd love to see him suffer at my hand. How dare he do this to us. How dare he hurt her, my Iris.

She's frightened, terrified. The tiny amount of bravado she had a few moments ago disappeared the second he tied her up, and I am powerless. We both are.

The smell of petrol is stronger now, filling the air around us. Its soaking into the carpet and furniture. Why is he prolonging the inevitable? Just fucking do it, Adam.

He takes a lighter from his pocket, flicks the top open and closed repeatedly. He's loving this. Loving every minute.

"I really didn't want it to come to this, George, but it's the only way."

I shake my head. It's all I can do. Iris's head is slumped. She's given up. It sounds like Jem has too. Her constant barking has turned to long, low, pitiful howls. She's crying. That's exactly what she's doing, and it's fucking heartbreaking.

Adam approaches me, flicking his lighter with every step. Our noses touch and I can smell alcohol on his breath.

He pockets the lighter, paces the room. Then he fumbles

with something on the inside of his jacket and pulls out what looks like a wad of envelopes.

"You see this?" he says, waving the elastic band wrapped bundle in my face.

I nod, but don't know why.

"These are letters."

"And?" Shit! I didn't mean to say that out loud.

"They're mine," he leers, "I wrote them. All of them. To you."

Adam starts to drop them, one by one, on to the floor around our chairs. I watch, mesmerized at the petrol seeping into their fibres.

Fuck.

"But you never read them, did you?" he says, voice breaking, "you got them, I know you did. But you threw them away, didn't you?"

Oh. My. God.

"Do you know how fucking hard it was for me, sneaking around, trying to find new places to leave them? Can you even comprehend the work that went into that?"

So, it was Adam. He sent the letters. Wow.

I loved those fucking letters. It was exciting. I had no one. Well, I have my parents, but I had no friends. I was a complete loner. I couldn't click with anyone at high school, or primary school, for that matter. I was happy in my own little world. I only needed my music and my books. They were my friends. They didn't argue with me. They didn't force my head in the toilet and pull the flush. They were just there. For me.

So, the letters were just something else. I felt wanted. I've had pen pals in the past, the result of a couple of foreign exchange students, but these letters, the secret, sexy ones that told me I was gorgeous, told me the writer wanted to do things with me that made me blush, well, they awoken something in me. Confidence. Yes, confidence. I wasn't the shit off someone's shoe anymore.

They were always pushed through the letterbox to begin with. The envelopes had my full name and address on them, and always a first-class stamp. I always wondered who, and where they were coming from because there was never a postmark, but that's as far as my wondering went.

But then they started appearing on my bedroom floor, in my rucksack, under my fucking pillow. And that's when things got even more exciting. The thought of someone gaining entry into your home, it should scare you, terrify you. I wasn't scared. I wasn't terrified. Far from it. It turned me on. I never told anyone about them. They were all mine. My little secret.

The letters started to fizzle out, and by the time I'd got through my first term at college, they'd stopped completely. It broke me, to be honest. I felt like a no one all over again.

Then I met two guys, who would go on to be my very best friends. I didn't think much about them after that. I was too busy having way too much fun.

And now, I've found out that one of them wanted to be way more than that.

I

Don't

Believe

This!

But I can, actually. It makes a lot of sense. Hindsight is good like that.

I never wanted to hurt Iris. No way. I thought my letters would excite her just as much as I used to be when I received mine. And I think she was when I first started sending them. She didn't seem scared, I don't think. More intrigued, I'd say. I should have stopped though, much earlier than I did. Especially once I knew how much they frightened her.

"It's going to hurt, George," Adam says, snapping me out of my reverie.

So what.

"It's going to hurt me as much as you. I loved you, George, I always will, but now I know the feeling isn't reciprocated. I know you'll only ever have eyes for her," he says, pointing his finger at her.

He paces the room, clearly thinking, but of what, I don't

know. He turns around to face us. He looks confused, flustered.

Iris whimpers in pain as he pulls the tape from her mouth and I brace myself as he rips mine away too. I inhale deeply.

"Adam, man, there's no need for this," I tell him.

"There's every need."

"No, there isn't," I say, but am interrupted by movement on my left-hand side. The door opens.

"Adam, stop!" Lucas shouts.

Iris lets out a muffled sound, part scream, part sigh of relief. I strain against my bindings and hope to God he's here to save us.

"What the hell are you doing here, Lucas?" Adam shouts.

"I followed you."

"Why? How?"

"I've been watching you, Adam. Following you. For weeks. I'll follow you forever."

"What the fuck?"

"Please, for me, just stop!"

"Stop? For you? What the hell are you going on about?"

"Don't say you don't know," Lucas says, pointing at himself.

"Know what?"

"I love you. I've always loved you. George on the other hand…"

I shoot a glance at Lucas. I don't love Adam, but Lucas doesn't exactly need to rub that in even further. Not right now.

Adam laughs heartily, but the laugh turns sour.

"Shut your fucking mouth, Lucas," he says, "you don't know shit!"

"I do. I know what you've been playing at. I know about the letters you've left for them," Lucas says, gesturing to us, "I know you've been breaking in."

"It's not breaking in if you've got a key," Adam grins, waving a set in the air.

I feel sick. I look at Iris, her eyes as wide as saucers.

"How?" Lucas asks what we can't.

"Oh, oh of course. You don't know, do you?" Adam looks at me, laughing.

What the fuck? What's he talking about?

"Know what?" I shout. This is getting ridiculous.

"My Mom. Your estate agent."

Shit!

"Just in case you need it spelling out, although, by the looks on your faces, I think we're all on the same page," Adam says, "you bought her house, our family home, of which I've always had keys for. I may not have lived there for ages, but it will always be my home."

"But... but how could I have missed this? How did I not know what you were up to? I've followed you everywhere!" Lucas says.

"Clearly not," Adam laughs.

"Why?" Iris asks.

"Why not?" he replies and then returns his interest back to Lucas, a look of realisation washing over his face.

"Anyway, why the fuck have you been following me, you loser?"

"Pot, kettle, black. I could ask you the same."

Adam looks straight at me, longingly.

"Oh. I get it," Lucas says, clearly hurt.

"No. You don't. You never will."

"Don't be so fucking patronising! You think you're the only person who loves someone who doesn't love you back?"

Adam is full of rage, all directed at Lucas. We've been given a reprieve.

"What are you talking about?"

"I know you love George. You've loved him for as long as we've all been together. It's so obvious it's sickening."

"Fuck you, Lucas!"

"What? Are you denying it?"

"No. George knows how I feel about him. I just told him. All of it."

"At least it's out there now. Maybe I should take a leaf out of your book."

Adam looks confused, but there's nothing cryptic in what Lucas is saying.

"You're not the only person who feels cheated."

"Jesus, Lucas, you're really starting to piss me off."

"You still don't get it, do you?"

Adam screams in frustration, lunges at him. Lucas somehow manages to grab hold of him, and all he can do is squirm.

Lucas forces his mouth onto Adam's, smothers him with it. Adam pulls back sharply, as shocked as us by his friends' outburst. He wipes his arm across his mouth.

"I love you, Adam. I know you don't feel the same about me, but there you go."

"You got that right," Adam replies, but looks straight at me.

Lucas turns to the door, walks up to it, locks it. He stands there, arms crossed.

"What the?" Adam shouts.

"What you're doing, whatever you're planning here, is wrong. Unforgivable. I can smell the petrol. The room is thick with it. Why would you want to kill someone you love?"

"Because I can't have him, that's why. And if I can't, no one can."

"I can't have you, either. So, let's do this. Let's all go out together. If you're going to blow this place up, we may as well all go up with it!"

It could be my eyes playing tricks on me, but I swear Lucas has just winked at me.

Adam turns his back to him, starts pacing like a caged animal.

Lucas looks at me and cocks his head, only very slightly, towards the kitchen window. I don't know what he's trying to get at, but as I steal the smallest glance in that direction, I see shadows moving. There are people out there. Police. I look back at Lucas. He nods.

"You know what? That's not such a bad idea," Adam says, flicking the lighter lid again, "I've got nothing left. The only person I've ever loved doesn't give a shit about me. What's the point in anything anymore?"

I want to tell Adam how stupid he's being, but the words won't come. I don't have the energy to form them. It wasn't me who distanced myself from him. He drew himself away from me. I did everything I could to save our friendship, but now I realise nothing would have worked because he wanted so much more, more than I'd ever be able to give him.

19

When Adam started pouring the petrol, I felt sick, terrified. The thought of never seeing George again, the thought of the heat, and pain – it's heartbreaking. But then in comes Lucas, and with him, a distraction, a break from it all. And there are people outside, people I'm guessing are police. Adam hasn't noticed them, yet.

I always thought there was something about him, and how he was around George. It felt like more than just a "bromance". And they were all so close, the three of them, until me and George became an item. But that shit happens, right? It's a natural progression. It's not like I took George away from them. He did his best to keep their friendship alive, but Adam made things difficult, not just for George, for Lucas too. Lucas stopped hanging out with us, but clung on to Adam, and his every word. No wonder he started having feelings for his best friend.

Adam's flicking the lid on the lighter again, facing me and George.

"Go on then, what are you waiting for?" Lucas shouts, "Do it!"

20

Adam pulls something from behind his back. It's a gun. Don't know what make or model. Don't need to. All I know is that this is it. This is the last time I'll ever see her, my Iris. I look at her, take her all in.

My ex best friend grins and points the gun at her. I can't. I can't see this. But I keep my eyes open. I keep them on her. She closes hers, bracing herself for the end.

BANG!

The sound makes me flinch and my eyes close instinctively. Then I hear breaking glass, and a sharp intake of breath, and that makes me open them again. I look at Iris. She opens her eyes and I follow her gaze as tears streak down her face. I don't know whether it's relief, or sadness, or both, but I'm crying too.

Somewhere in the background, I hear Jem barking again. They may be a little muted, but it's clear to hear that she is not happy.

Adam's eyes are wide open, fixed on mine. I can't tell if it's a grimace or a grin that spreads slightly across his face, but there's no mistaking the last words that leave his mouth.

"I love you."

21

Police swarm our living room, rushing around, tending to us, and Adam's still body. I can't hear them although I know there's noise. Nothing is registering. No sound. Silence.

I'm crying but I don't know if it's because I'm relieved or sad. Maybe it's a mixture of both.

I can hear Jem again, barking frantically, madly. The sound maybe a little muffled, but there's no mistaking that she's not at all happy.

I look at George. He's crying too. Two officers are helping us out of our bindings, and, as if on cue, we throw our arms around each other and hug like we've never hugged before.

"I…" he begins, more tears welling up in his eyes.

"I know."

And I do know. Not that this has ever happened to me before, but I know that, in one fell swoop, he's lost his best friend, albeit one who came here to kill him, us.

Lucas is slumped on the floor, looking just as bewildered as we are. His eyes are wide, unblinking. He's not taken the kind of beating that we have, nothing physical anyway, but he's not okay. He's far from it. A paramedic takes his arm, gently helps him to stand and tells us all we're being taken to hospital. He point-blank refuses. So do we, and even though it's the last place I want to be right now, I know we need to go.

The adrenaline and shock have dampened the pain I'm in, for now, but the reality is, I feel like I've been trampled underfoot by a herd of elephants and that pain is only going to get worse.

We're quickly checked over, but this is just a temporary measure.

What about Jem? We can't leave her all alone.

"We've got a dog. She's upstairs, we think. Somewhere in the house, anyway," I tell the paramedic.

"Yes, she's been locked in one of the rooms. We can't leave her."

"You need to come to the hospital. You're both in a bad way," the paramedic replies.

"Let's just find her first, and then we'll think about what happens next," George demands, as calmly as he can.

Jem runs up to us. She's smiling, her mouth stretched from ear to ear. We brace ourselves for the hit, the excited pounce, but it's as if she knows she must be gentle. She knows we're hurt.

We form a physical bond, the three of us, but we're going to have to break it. She can't come with us to the hospital.

We can't phone the rescue centre because it's closed, but we can't leave her. Who knows how long we'll be away?

"I've got it!" George shouts, pulling out of our circle.

"What?" I cry.

George turns to the paramedic and explains that the owner of the pub knows us, and Jem, that we frequent it regularly, and could they ask him if he wouldn't mind dog-sitting whilst we're away from home, however long that may be.

"We'll see what we can do," the paramedic says, stroking Jem's head.

George thanks her, close to tears. I can't speak. This hurts way more than the physical pain I'm in.

"You know we can't promise anything, but I'll do my best to make sure she's looked after until you return."

We close ranks with Jem once more, hug her as tightly as our injuries will allow, and hope beyond all hope that the paramedic is true to her word.

We're escorted to two ambulances. Lucas is helped into one, George and I into another. I asked if we could stay together. I'll never leave his side again.

LUCY ONIONS

22

Police swarm the living room, rushing around, tending to us and Adam's deadly still body. I've never seen anyone being zipped up into a body bag, well, not in real life anyway, and certainly not when the body is that of a friend, a best friend. That's what he is, was. What he did to me is wrong, what he came to do, totally unforgivable. To think I put Iris through the very same thing, well it makes me as bad as him, so really, who am I to be angry about the letters, the sneaking, the stalking?

Would he have done it? Would he have torched us all to the ground? Would he have shot us all, one by one? Was he bluffing? We'll never know.

I look over at Lucas, he still looks shell-shocked. If it wasn't for his quick thinking, his actions, we'd all be dead.

I put my arms around his shaking shoulders, his sobs are deep and painful.

Two paramedics approach us. One of them takes Lucas's arm and gently helps him to stand up. He doesn't want to go to hospital, he point-blank refuses.

"Come on, Lucas," I tell him, "none of us really want to go, but it's good to be on the safe side, huh?"

"It's fine, honest. It's you two who need to go, not me.

I'm not hurt."

He may not be physically, but mentally, this will have done a good job on him.

I insist. He's not getting out of this.

"We need to stick together," Iris agrees, hugging us both.

5

1

It feels like a new house all over again. The smell of petrol is gone. Almost. I can still detect a hint of it. George and Lucas haven't seemed to notice it so maybe it's my brain playing tricks on me. Maybe I'll never completely get rid of it, the feeling, the smell.

Lucas only stayed overnight at hospital just for observation purposes. He came away with a clean bill of health, albeit only physical. He's still struggling with it all. We all are. Me and George, on the other hand, well, we had a lengthier stay.

George's injuries beat mine into the ground. Two broken ribs, a bust-up nose, delayed concussion and fractured clavicle. I got off more lightly with a sprained wrist, mild concussion and whiplash. Things could have been so much worse.

We were, the three of us, put up over the road, at the pub. The owner allowed us to stay for free, told us he would do anything he could to help us. I cried when he said that, even more when he said how good Jem had been, and that he'd happily look after her again if need be. I couldn't believe how thoughtful the offer was and my faith in humanity was somewhat restored, but after a few days, we all felt bad about not paying our way. So, for the remaining couple of days, we clubbed together and settled the bill. I'm sure they didn't charge us full price though.

Whilst we were staying at the pub, I arranged for the house to be fumigated, and for all the living room furniture to be reupholstered, and now we're here again, back in our home. And it smells like my candles and my washing. And yes, Lucas is here too and he's staying. After everything we've been through, I wanted him to know that he had a home with us, his friends.

My stomach churns, rumbles like rolling thunder. I haven't eaten since yesterday afternoon.

I turn the grill on and grab a pack of smoked bacon from the fridge. I lay all eight slices out on the grill tray. I'm salivating (almost as much as Jem) just thinking about how good they're going to taste.

The rashers begin to pop and sizzle, filling the kitchen, and the living room, with their unmistakable smell. Coupled with the coffee aroma, I almost forget about recent events.

I hear movement upstairs.

Jem's tail beats the floor in excitement, but she's not moving an inch. There's no way she's about to take her eyes off our breakfast.

George appears first, greets me with a hug from behind. His chin nestles into the crook of my neck, and his breath tickles me, gives me goosebumps.

He strokes Jem's head.

"Hey," his voice comes out a drawl.

I turn around and kiss him.

"Did you sleep?" he mumbles.

I shake my head.

"Why don't you go up now? Go and get some rest."

"I'll sleep when I'm ready, and I'm not right now, so I thought I'd do something useful."

George smiles. I heard him snoring, but even so, he looks like he hasn't slept for years. I tell him about the cleaners, how

I want to get everything back to normal. As if getting rid of the smell will make everything okay again.

"Well, if they come again today, I'll stay here whilst they're doing what they do. You go out and get some fresh air."

"I'm not going anywhere. I'm staying with you. I don't think we should be apart."

He pulls me into him, kisses the top of my head.

I plate our food up and leave one in the still warm oven for Lucas.

We eat greedily to the sound of Jem's smacking chops.

Lucas pops his head round the wall, greets us sleepily.

"There's some breakfast in the oven," George manages to say through a mouthful of food.

"Thanks," he yawns.

An uncomfortable silence falls between us. Of course it's going to feel awkward.

"I need to show you something," Lucas says.

"Oh?" George replies, attention piqued.

"Yeah. Eat up, we're going out."

2

Adam was the first of us to move out of our respective, childhood homes. The first to fly the nest. I don't know whether he was pushed, or if he left of his own accord, but by age nineteen, he was in his own pad, and being here, right now, is bringing back so many awesome memories. We were a team, the three of us, a gang, and we spent many days, and nights, here. Being here without him, well it feels wrong.

"I'm not sure I like this. It doesn't seem right," I say.

"I know," Lucas frowns, tears pricking his eyes.

"So, what's with the walk down memory lane?" I say, rubbing his back in an effort to console him.

"If it was only that simple," he says, "George, I don't think you realise how badly it got to him when you got with Iris."

Iris coughs uncomfortably, and I can see her grip growing tighter on Jem's lead. I get the feeling she'd rather be anywhere else but here, right now. I can't say I disagree with her.

"When you left," Lucas continues, "Adam asked me to leave too. He said that nothing could ever be the same again. He said I'd be the last remains of such good times and that he couldn't deal with being reminded of it all every time he looked at me. I told him he was being silly. Told him that I hadn't done anything wrong. But I left. It hurt so much to go, but it would have hurt even more for me to stay somewhere I really wasn't wanted."

"Mate, I'm sorry. I am. But I hadn't done anything wrong either had I, Lucas? Unless you think getting a girlfriend is wrong."

"No, it's not wrong and I know that, but at the time, I blamed you even more than I blamed him because I was obsessed with him. I wanted him to love me as much as I loved him. As much as he loved you. When he realised he'd lost you forever…"

"He didn't lose me. I just got a girlfriend," I look at Iris, and realising I sound a little harsh, I apologise. Tell her it wasn't meant to come out like that.

"When you hooked up with Iris, then, he knew he'd never get you back, so he asked me to move back in. I suppose he thought it better to have someone that no one at all. And like some pathetic, spineless dick, I agreed."

"If he was so sad and lonely, he could have got rid of the flat and moved back in with his Mum, Lucas. It's not like he had no one at all."

"Would you have done that? Seriously? Come on, George. Imagine having all that freedom, that independence and then giving it all up. It's not exactly moving on, is it?"

I shake my head. He's right. It would feel like giving up.

"And I didn't just agree to move back in, I jumped at the chance! Anything to be closer to him was all good by me. I think we both needed that, someone permanent."

I think that's a dig at me. No, I'm sure it is.

"Sorry, that sounds harsh, but it's the truth. I'm sorry if that upsets you."

"Don't worry about it," I say, shaking my head.

"But, over time, he began to shut himself away," Lucas says, looking at the floor, "He became withdrawn, not just from me, from everyone, everything."

"I did wonder why he stopped coming to work," Iris says quietly, looking at me.

"Yeah. You know he handed his notice in, right?"

I shake my head.

Iris does too.

"Not even I knew his plans. He told me afterwards, said I wasn't to tell anyone. I was so worried about him. He put bolts and locks on the outside of his bedroom door. He didn't want anyone in there, and to me, that could only mean he was trying to hide something.

"Then, on the night it happened, he seemed agitated, nervy even. He was rushing around all over the place. He told me he was going out and he didn't know when he'd be back. It was all really weird.

"I went upstairs to have a shower, and I noticed he'd left his door open. I told myself I mustn't go into his room, but it was too much to resist."

Lucas pauses, takes a breath.

"Well?" we both ask him.

"I couldn't believe what I was seeing, it seemed unreal. But it all made total sense too, and call it instinct, but I knew exactly where he'd gone. I called the police straight away. I didn't want him to get into trouble, even though I knew he undoubtedly would, I just knew whatever he was planning on doing needed to be stopped. I felt like I was betraying him at the time, but I know now that I did the right thing.

My head starts to shake but feels like it's not me controlling the movement. I feel like I'm not in my own body. The muscles around my mouth slacken as it drops open. I'm not going to add to Lucas's upset by telling him that Adam had been drinking with me, that up until the moment he took me to that basement, lock up, whatever it was, and beat the living crap out of me, we'd been having a great night, and that it felt good to be back with my best friend again.

No, I'm not going to tell him that. It would ruin him.

"You need to see. Come on," he says.

I grip Iris's hand, and she squeezes mine back. She's as white as a ghost, and I feel queasy, off balance. Jem doesn't seem too happy either. I don't know what we're going to find but I know it's not going to be good.

Iris pulls me back as we reach the top of the stairs. Lucas's hand hovers over the door handle.

"I don't like this," she says.

3

I can't stop the sharp, shocked, intake of breath. George is frozen, stunned to silence, like a deer in the headlights of a speeding car. Lucas can't look at us, the floor seems far more interesting.

Adam's room is on lockdown. There's police tape stretched across the door, and behind the yellow and black plastic, officers are dusting for prints, taking photos, recording everything. We're told that this is now a crime scene, and we're not permitted to enter, although, as it's Lucas's home, he's allowed access to all other rooms.

There are photos everywhere, and even though I can't get any closer to them, it's not hard to make out that they're all of George.

I spot one particular photo, of the three friends together and start to cry. There will never be a reenactment of this, of these best friends, laughing. George's life, Lucas's life, will never be the same again. Because for all I'm hating Adam for what he has done, they had a bond. One they thought was unbreakable.

I'm in some of the photos, but I've been scratched out, or replaced with Adam's smiling image. I'm almost thinking that the photos look better without me, as if George looks happier with Adam by his side. I blink away these thoughts along with my tears.

There must be hundreds of photos. Has to be.

This isn't right.

This is scary.

This is a shrine.

4

I can't take my eyes off Iris. I'm watching her watching the police. I glance at the scene in front of me, of police dusting for prints, taking photos, recording every detail of the crime scene. The only thing that separates us from them is yellow and black tape, stretched across the door frame. Almost reminds me of Halloween. We were big on it, me, Adam and Lucas. Looked forward to it more than Christmas. Man, we threw some parties.

There are photos everywhere, of me, and me and her. Too many to count.

And then reality hits me like an electric shock.

This is not right.

This is seriously fucking wrong.

This is a shrine.

5

I can hear George asking me not to cry, almost pleading with me, but his voice isn't loud. It's like he's calling me from miles away. I know he's here with me, but I feel like he's on another planet, a faraway world. Or maybe he's a memory, a subconscious thought, maybe. This isn't real. It can't be. I mean, it feels real, but...

My head feels like it's spinning, spiraling out of control. My heart is beating way too fast, so fast it's hurting. I place my hand over it, will it to slow down. Beads of sweat are dripping from my nose and stinging my eyes. I want to scream, shout. I'm going to explode.

"Iris!" George says, this time bringing me right back into the room. He wraps his arms around me, "Iris, it's okay. We're okay."

I close my eyes, squeeze them shut, as if there's a bomb about to go off. My body shakes, tremors ripple through me, and finally, I breathe in, fill my lungs with air. I inhale greedily and exhale slowly, steadily. I start to cry again and wonder if I'll ever stop.

6

Iris's shaking body almost makes me do the same, but I've got to be everything she needs right now. I've got to be strong, unshakeable, even though inside, I'm a mess. I feel her relax within my grasp, feel her let go a little. That's better, Iris. There, there. It doesn't take a degree in rocket science to figure she's had a panic attack. I should know, I've had enough of them. It's textbook.

I spot one of the police officers holding something up with a pair of tweezers, about to slip it into a plastic evidence bag. It's a letter.

"Excuse me, could I see that please?" I ask, in no way expecting a favourable response.

She seals the bag, takes a few steps towards us. She tells us that she can't allow us to touch it as it's evidence, but holds it out in front of her, understanding I want to read it.

I've written many letters in my time, to pen pals, to foreign exchange students, and more recently to the love of my life, my best friend, George. Those were quite covert and sneaky. Exciting, even. This letter is unlike any I've ever written. It's the last I'll ever write.

I've always wondered what it would feel like to pen my suicide note.

I need wonder no more. This is it.

But that's not all this is. It's also to say I won't be leaving this world alone. I'm taking the love of my life, my best friend, George with me.

I can't leave knowing that he and his girlfriend, Iris, will live the rest of their lives in total, loved up bliss. So, I'll obviously have to kill her too because, you know, they're a "partnership" now and they literally do everything *together. Sickening really. Anyway, if it means it's the only way I can take him with me, then so be it. Needs must and all that.*

See ya,
Adam xxx

7

From the look on George's face, I know that whatever is on that paper, in that letter, is not good.

"Piece of shit!" George seethes, eyes full of anger.

"Let me see," I say.

Lucas comes up beside me. We start to read.

"Motherfucker!" Lucas whispers and walks away.

My mouth falls open in shock. How can one side of lined paper strike such a cruel blow?

I don't think I've ever hated anyone. There are people I dislike, but hate? Well, it's a sharp, strong word. It can make you bitter. Then there's Adam. What he's done is despicable, and for once, even though he's not here for me to say it to his face, I can honestly, truly say I hate him,

EPILOGUE

Here we are. I never thought we'd be doing this, standing around an open grave, waiting for Adam's coffin to be lowered into it. Not given the circumstances of it, and certainly not this early on in life.

What he did, what he'd been doing, was awful. I know that because I did exactly the same. But I stopped, didn't let it get that far.

Adam wanted to kill me, us. That's one thing I'll never ever get over. But he was blinded by the love he felt for me. He wasn't thinking straight. Or maybe he was. Maybe it was the surest he'd ever been about anything in his life. I don't know. But somewhere, down the line, he was my best friend, and I don't think I'll ever forget that.

Iris didn't want to come. She said she understood why I needed to be here, but that she would feel a hypocrite if she did, but I told her how much I needed her to support me today, and at that, she didn't think twice.

Adam's Mum, our estate agent, hasn't made eye contact with us. If I were in her shoes, I'd be the same. She's not crying, but she looks broken, exhausted. I can't imagine how she must be feeling. To lose her only child, in the way she has, and for the reason she has, must, I suppose, be one hell of a mindfuck. I mean, how would you even process that?

Lucas looks blank. He's the one I feel the sorriest for in all of this. He's been a constant companion to Adam, through everything. That's love.

Love blinds you, takes away your peripheral vision, leaving you to see only what is straight in front of you. You're oblivious to faults and flaws. It's all consuming, unconditional.

As the Reverend commits Adam to the earth, I feel a lump forming in my throat. Tears fill my eyes and I'm thinking that, even after everything he's done, to all three of us, he was once the best friend I ever had. I'm angry, devastated. I'm torn.

I look at Iris and she looks back, a small, sympathetic smile on her lips. She nods, silently letting me know she understands, telling me, without words, that we're going to be alright.

And we will.

I know we will.

Always.

ALWAYS

ACKNOWLEDGMENTS

To my husband, Simon. I wouldn't be me without you. I couldn't do this without you. Thanks, bab.

To my daughter, Molly. You amaze me, and you're my proudest achievement ever. You're a one off and I love you so, so much. Never change.

To my Mum and Dad, thank you for always telling it like it is. Your love, support and encouragement mean the world to me. Where would I be without you both? Thanks for being the best grandparents ever, too.

To my little Sister, and my very best friend, Ella. You are one in a million, one of a kind. I don't know what I'd do without you. You're the coolest Aunty ever.

To my two favourite little boys, Max and Harry – you're both as crazy as a box of frogs, and that's why I love you both lots. Even more than cheese.

To my brother in law, and fellow soul singer, Paul – you're alright too, I suppose!

To BB, my crazy, rockin', next door neighbour and best mate. You truly are amazing and just as mental as me.

To Kearon, I may not be your Mum, but I'm super proud of you. And you're also good for swapping comics with.

To Leigh, the man who has to deal with my nutter of a best friend. You're a legend.

Huge thanks to all my fellow authors and book club buddies (particularly Paul, Rachel and Sue, for all their help). I love the fact that we go off on tangents and that, most importantly, we just *get* each other regardless of whatever we're jabbering on about.

Special thanks to the awesome, James Josiah. Thanks for editing, for listening. Thanks for your advice and for believing in me. Thanks for being the other half of our awesome, Black Dream, and of course, just for being bloody brilliant.

Last, but by no means least, I have to say thanks for the music and bands that have provided the perfect writing

389

soundtrack for Always. Thanks to The Beatles, Bowie, Carole King, Fleetwood Mac, Gerard Way, frnk iero and the cellabration (deliberate spelling mistake, that's actually the name of the band), Haim, James, Jack Savoretti, James Bay, Lana Del Rey, My Chemical Romance, Nirvana, Pearl Jam, Prince, Soundgarden, The Used, and many more. The list could go on and on. I'm not joking.

A NOTE FROM THE AUTHOR

I found the first ever novella I wrote, not so long back. I remember the day I wrote it, then typed it up on the portable typewriter my Nan had bought me for either that Christmas or my birthday. I was at senior school. I'm not sure if that's true. My brain plays tricks on me. A lot. But it's such a strong, vivid memory. I remember changing the ink cartridge. I remember the click-clacking of the keys, the zip and bing of starting a new line. So, on that basis, I'm classing this as a real, tangible memory.

I remember thinking, at the time of writing it, that it would be a dream come true to be able to see my words printed on the pages of a real book, not just on a pile of paper. My love for reading knew no bounds, it still doesn't, and I wondered what it would feel like for my writing to affect others, just like the writing of my favourite authors affected me.

Twenty-seven years on, I can now proudly say that I've got (including the book you've literally just finished) four books to my name. And people have read them, reviewed them. My words have affected my readers in some way, and that is, quite honestly, an amazing, humbling feeling. I may not have made my fortune (yet), but you ask any author worth their salt, and they'll all say the same. It's not about the money. If it was, we'd have given up by now.

We write because we must, because these characters and stories flying around in our heads won't rest until they find their new home, as scribblings on paper, or whatever medium we have to hand at that time. We may not be able to spend every waking moment writing, but that is life and it's the life I love, and I wouldn't have it any other way.

ABOUT THE AUTHOR

Lucy Onions hails from sunny Walsall in the West Midlands. She resides in a 2-bed, semi-detached with her husband, Simon, her daughter, Molly and a Staffordshire Bull Terrier called Rosie.

When she's not writing, Lucy is a photographer (**www.lucyonionsphotography.com**), a lead singer (**www.souldoutuk.com**) and she runs a lovely little book-club called Walsall Book Social. She's also one half of the publishing imprint that brings this book to you, Black Dream. which all means she's always stupidly busy but that's the way she rock 'n' rolls.

She hopes you've enjoyed reading the book as much as she did writing it. She'd love it even more if you left her a little review of it. Somewhere.

If you would like to find out any more about her writing and what's coming up next, you can find out more here:
www.facebook.com/LucyOnionsAuthor

Printed in Poland
by Amazon Fulfillment
Poland Sp. z o.o., Wrocław